Scoring with Sadie

A Fake Dating Enemies To Lovers Sports Romance

Chiquita Dennie

304 Publishing Company

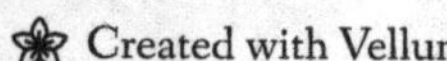 Created with Vellum

Introduction

Grab some wine and get ready for more spicy, sinful, sexy suspense.

Are you signed up for my newsletter?

Join today for all the latest new releases, contests, giveaways, sneak peeks, and more.

www.chiquitadennie.com

Disclaimer

This work of fiction contains strong language and explicit sexual content and is only intended for mature readers. This story may contain unconventional situations, language, and sexual encounters that may offend some readers. This book is for mature readers (18+).

Latest Releases

Until Serena (HEA World Novel)
Antonio and Sabrina: Struck in Love 5
Heart of Stone, Book 4 (Jessica and Joseph)
She's All I Need
Red Light District (A Fantasy Romance Short)
Claim: The Carrington Cartel Book 2
Joaquin Fuertes (The Fuertes Cartel Book 3)
Something Gained (A Romantic Comedy Book 1)
Scoring with Sadie
Upcoming Releases (2023/2024):
Fall For You (Satin Hill Book 1)
Nicco: TN Seal Security Book 3
Something Earned (A Romantic Comedy Book 2)

Synopsis

Destin

I'm not only the star player on the Tennessee Panthers team; I'm bringing the team back to the finals cup. It doesn't help when I clash with the coach, and the management team assigns a new physical therapist who thinks she knows everything. She keeps reminding me that the final decision if I ever play again is up to her. I need to figure out whether I listen to my gut or Sadie. Do I risk further damage to my leg or put my heart at risk?

Sadie

As the daughter of the coach and the new physical therapist, I've had to prove myself for years to get to where I am. When the opportunity to become the new therapist for the Tennessee Panthers opens up, I jump at the chance. The only problem is Destin pushing back on my every suggestion to get him back into the game.

Will Sadie and Destin compromise and realize it's better to work together? Or will the enemies crash and burn before the cup finals start?

Chapter 1

Destin

"**D**estin, over here!" A bright flash went off in my face as I shoved the paparazzi out of my way and stumbled out of the club. The bottle girl I picked up giggled and groped my dick as another flash went off.

"Who's the lucky lady, Destin?" the reporter called out.

Annoyed and ready to get to a hotel, I grunt, "None of your business."

I made it to my red Charger and helped the bottle girl in before jogging to the driver's side.

"Come on, Destin. Let's give them a show," she whispered, kissing me behind the ear.

Most of the time, the men in my field liked the media attention and the women hanging on their every word. I was on the verge of being the latest fuck up in the sports world, and that would only end one way—with me in jail or dead from not giving a fuck.

I revved the engine and turned on the headlights to get the photographers to move so I could leave. The bottle girl rubbed my chest, but I moved my head when she tried to kiss me on the lips. It was after midnight, and she was trying to make a show for the cameras.

"You know better," I muttered.

She pouted and rolled her eyes. Every woman wanted to be my permanent girl because it came with money, status, and celebrity.

Finally on the road, I checked the mirror to see a few cars following, trying to snap pictures. I complained all the time, and they still followed. I smirked and decided to have a little fun with them.

"Fasten your seatbelt."

She smiled and sat up to look behind her, seeing the photographers with their cameras out of the window. "We have company."

I pressed my foot on the gas. "We do."

She reached over and unfastened my belt, palming my dick. "Should we give them a show?"

My back stiffened. "Shit, girl!"

Licking her lips, she lowered her head and took my entire length into her mouth like a vacuum.

"Fuck!" I accidentally pulled my foot from the gas pedal, vaguely aware of sirens in the background.

"Mmm...." she moaned as my hand fell on her neck.

The sirens grew louder. "Shit. The cops."

She sat up abruptly, and I pulled over, tucking my dick back into my pants as she got herself together.

A flashlight blinded me through the driver's window as I rolled it down.

"Get back! No cameras!" the officer yelled.

My head fell back with a groan, knowing I was about to be in the newspapers all over the world.

"Do you know why I've stopped you?" the officer asked.

"I wasn't speeding."

"No, but you were swerving all over the place," he responded.

"Do you know who you're talking to?" The girl whose name I'd forgotten blurted.

I shushed her as the police officer directed his flashlight into the car to get a better look at us.

"Another rich boy with no regard for anyone else on the road," he spat.

I locked my hands around the steering wheel. "Man, just give me a ticket so we can go."

"Step out of the vehicle."

"For what?"

"Out of the car, now!"

"This is bullshit." I cut the engine.

I knew what this was—an officer on a power trip, trying to make a name for himself by hauling me out of the car. A high-profile lock-up like me would be all over the media before I even had my rights read.

I glanced at the bottle girl, huddled close to the window. I started to snatch the phone from her hand when the door was yanked open, and the night went from bad to worse.

* * *

I groaned as a kick to my bed woke me.

"I leave town for one weekend, and you get arrested?"

The loud voice ringing in my ears was the one person I wanted to avoid before it hit the news stations.

"Get up!"

Another kick to my bed as the sun slammed into my eyes. I used the pillow to block out the blinding rays. "Close the goddamn blinds."

Elise grabbed the pillow and yanked it off my head.

"You're fired," I growled.

"Well, that would be wonderful, but no one else wants to work with you. If you want to fight my husband because you're being a jerk and firing his wife, be my guest."

I opened one eye to see her sitting on the couch in the corner of my bedroom, smirking as she typed on her phone.

"Can you give me some privacy?" I motioned to my lower half, covered by the blanket.

Elise snorted. "Please! The whole world has seen that little shrimp." She pretended to throw up as she rose from the couch. "Get dressed and meet me downstairs."

"Why? I wasn't charged. We're good since I'm not in the system."

"You may have gotten off with the courts, but the public knows you were spotted with a prostitute."

I waved off her comment. "She was a bottle girl."

"She's trying to sell the story. Now, shower and meet me downstairs," Elise instructed, marching out of my room.

Yawning, I sat up and checked the time on my watch. I'd only had about four hours of sleep.

The cops didn't book me, thank God. The officer who pulled me over took me in, but a few of the cops at the stations were fans, so I got off with a warning when I took selfies, signed autographs, and promised to visit a wedding.

Stomping to the bathroom, I turned on the shower and grabbed a fresh towel. Elise showing up meant Coach Lester and the management team had found out before I could explain. Elise had been my publicist for two years since my first one quit when I told her we couldn't be together. She'd wanted more, and I had no plans to settle down as a husband or a father. My only goal in life was playing and winning championships.

Freshly showered, I dressed in jogging pants and a t-shirt and picked up my gym bag. I strolled downstairs to find Elise in the kitchen eating my breakfast.

"Don't you have a home to eat at?" I snatched a piece of bacon from her plate.

She smacked my hand. "Stop, fool. I'm pregnant and need my breakfast."

"Shouldn't you have that at home?"

"Shut up and sit." Elise gestured at the stool next to her.

Laughter from my housekeeper caught my attention. Tilting my head, I glared at her for constantly taking Elise's side in our arguments. "You selling out on me, too, Shelly?"

Shelly had been my housekeeper for six years since I moved into this place following my team's last win. My parents didn't live far from me, and my mother constantly worried about me eating right, so she talked with one of her church friends. Shelly retired as a home health care worker at sixty-four.

"Leave Elise alone and eat your breakfast. You have practice soon." Shelly put a full plate of my favorite morning foods in front of me—bacon, grits, toast, and fruit.

"You made my protein shake?"

"Yes, don't I always?" Shelly shook the bottle in my face.

"He's so spoiled," Elise muttered.

I flicked her nose, and she punched my arm. Elise got on my nerves, but I treated her like a sister and would hurt anyone who tried to hurt her. Marrying Sean, my best friend on the team, we'd been around each other for years. When she told me about starting her own public relations firm, I jumped on board when the scandal with my last publicist had me plastered all over social media.

"Whatever, girl." I roll my neck and snap my fingers the way she does with her girlfriends.

She pins me with a no-nonsense glare. "You need to get ahead of this story."

"What is the story?"

"Haven't you checked social media?" Elise scrolled on her phone and placed it on the counter.

"*Tennessee Panthers Starting Player Arrested with Prostitute.*" I shook my head vigorously as I read the headline aloud.

"Coach called me early this morning and wants you in practice, followed by a meeting with management," Elise said.

I pushed her phone back to her. "First, she's not a prostitute."

Elise gulped the rest of her orange juice. "If you say that one more time, I'm going to slap you." She stood as I finished my breakfast. "I need you to be on your best behavior, Destin."

I downed my protein shake, wiped my mouth with the napkin, and slipped on my shades. "Aren't I always?"

Elise smacked me on the back of the head, answering her phone as I opened the door to leave.

I noticed her car parked crooked next to mine. "If you hit my car, I'm suing you, girl."

"My husband says shut up," Elise snickered as I opened the passenger door of my Bentley for her.

I tossed my bag on the backseat. "I know how much he makes. He can't talk."

I grinned as she flipped me off and started the car, heading out of the gated community toward the stadium.

Chapter 2

Sadie

"I'm telling you, Sadie, we need to do private lessons." George stared up at me, brushing a hand over his wavy hair.

As one of the players on the Panthers soccer team, he wasn't the first to flirt with me. Every time we had an appointment, he tried to sneak in a private session conversation. I turned him down every time because, to him, private sessions would be me naked on my back with his head between my legs.

I prided myself on being professional when I got this position as Assistant Director of Physical Therapy. For so long, I was overlooked because I didn't fit this business's typical physical therapist image. It was a male-dominated world, and women were afterthoughts in their knowledge of how to heal players.

My credentials and the degree and dedication I put in at college should have had them wanting to hire me right out of college, but it took a few years. Starting my own practice was my eventual goal, but this job on my father's team would allow me to work my way up to the position of physical therapist in charge. Then I planned to make the switch to private practice. After years of being around egos and self-absorbed alpha males, I would need a change.

I flipped through George's charts from his last session. I'd signed him up for more light work on his leg. "George, how many times do I have to tell you? It will never happen."

"Sadie, we'd be good together, girl." George reached for my hand as the door flew open, causing us both to jump.

"George, you better not be flirting with my daughter," Coach Lester barked, stalking to the weights and grabbing a few items.

My stomach grew tight, and my palms were sweaty at my father's constant interruptions. He always thought something was going on in my appointments.

"Coach, you know Sadie's safe with me." George threw his hands in the air.

"Boy, your own momma ain't safe with you," Coach fired back.

I dropped my head in embarrassment. This was one of the downsides of working with my father. No one was good enough for me, and he constantly tried to control my life.

I held up my hand. "Coach, can I help you with something?" He was now okay with me calling him coach like everybody else, but it had taken a little time.

"No, I needed to grab a few weights," he answered, taking off toward my equipment area.

"Can you do that after my sessions, please?" I motioned to the door.

"Sadie, I'm still your father..." Coach started his usual spiel.

I knew this would lead to another argument. I'd had enough of him making me feel like a little girl when I was a grown woman living independently and paying my bills.

I forced a smile and tapped George on the shoulder, indicating he should sit up. "George, can we reschedule for tomorrow?"

George frowned. "Are you sure?"

Nodding, I helped him to stand and passed him his crutches. "Positive. Remember to keep it easy on your left leg." I wagged a finger in his face. We were working on slowly getting him back into shape for the field after surgery on his knee.

George grinned. "Thanks, Sadie."

"Anytime." I waved goodbye and turned to glare at my father.

"You're welcome," he said.

I squared my shoulders. "For what? Interrupting my session?"

Coach released a heavy sigh. "Girl, you act just like your momma."

I poked out my lip and stomped my foot like the kid he thought I was. "Momma told you to stop barging in on my sessions."

"Wake up, Sadie. George is in the middle of a divorce. You should be thanking me."

"It's not like I'm dating him. He's my patient."

"Good, because it's your job on the line if you're seen dating the athletes. Besides, it makes me look bad." As usual, he left without hearing me out.

I covered my face with my hands and screamed.

Feeling a little better, I wandered over to my desk and checked my calendar for the rest of the day, seeing it was clear. "No appointments. Great, I can have lunch."

A year at the job came with a few perks, but I didn't rely on favoritism. I wanted to get to the top based on my skills. As a black woman in the business, it was hard enough to get an interview for a role, let alone hired.

My phone rang as I locked my office. Pulling it from my purse, I bumped into something solid, and my phone hit the ground.

"Watch where you're going!" a gruff voice snapped.

"Excuse you!" I huffed, picking up my phone and looking at the boulder I'd collided with.

Great. Destin Gray. The universe was working against me today. I was aggravated with everybody and still had three more hours of work.

"Sorry, Sadie!" Elise yelled over her shoulder.

I had no idea how she put up with Destin Gray's arrogant ass. He thought he was the greatest thing since sliced bread. Although to be honest, he was—visually, at least.

Six feet plus, with a bald head and long legs. Broad chest, wide shoulders, thickly veined forearms, and clean nails. I liked a man who cared for his nails, but Destin Gray pissed me off and turned me on in equal measure. His brown skin and chiseled jawline sucked in all the girls who only wanted to drop their panties for him.

I didn't dare fall for his type, no matter how much he thought I wanted him. No way in hell I'd sleep with a man like him. There weren't enough Casamigos in the world.

"Hey, what took you so long?" my friend, Kelly, questioned when I finally lifted my phone to my ear.

I shook off the encounter, knowing I only had an hour

to get food and head back to the office. "Sorry, my phone dropped on the ground."

"How's work going?"

"Trying to grab some food before my lunch is over," I replied, waiting for the elevator to hit my floor.

"Any cute players need support today?"

I laughed as I pushed the elevator button again, noticing my father and Destin arguing from the corner of my eye. "Behaving like asses," I muttered.

"Who?"

"Huh?"

"You said behaving like asses. Who's being an ass to you?"

Kelly was my ride-or-die. I loved that about her, but sometimes it left us in certain situations—like back in college when she caught her boyfriend cheating and wanted me to help her put sugar in his tank. It would have worked if she hadn't recorded the whole thing and posted it online, resulting in us being reprimanded.

"Destin's dumb ass," I mumbled.

His gaze met mine, and he glared at me as if he'd heard me. My eyes widened, and I hurried onto the elevator, laughing at myself. "Shit."

"What's wrong?"

"Girl, I called him an ass under my breath, but I think he heard me."

"Destin's sexy. I don't know why you're holding out."

"Please wash your eyes out."

"He's a chocolate drop I wouldn't mind letting melt in my mouth," Kelly teased.

My stomach turned queasy. "Think I'm going to be sick."

"Oh, please. You're in love with that man."

"All right. Time to clock back in. Talk later, Kelly."

She cackled as I hung up on her idiotic observation and tossed my phone into my purse. I got off the elevator and headed to the restaurant up the street where I usually went for lunch on a Friday.

* * *

As I drove home that evening, I stopped at the store for the ingredients to make my favorite salmon and rice bowl and to grab ice cream. I was good and cozy in my apartment after dinner watching TV when the doorbell rang.

"Drop the spoon and turn around." Kelly pointed at my favorite chocolate mint ice cream.

I groaned as she took it from my hands and put it back in the freezer.

Kelly was dressed in her sexy man-catcher outfit of a leather jumpsuit and was ready to go out. I wanted to stay home and catch up on Abbott Elementary. I hadn't planned to do anything other than relax on my one weekend off away from all the assholes at work.

"I had plans for that ice cream." I folded my arms.

"When's the last time you said yes?"

"Repeat that."

Kelly tosses the spoon in the sink. "Shonda Rhimes said yes for an entire year, and things started to change in her life."

I threw my hands up in the air. "Good for Shonda."

"You should try it. You might find someone instead of being stuck in the apartment on a Friday night." Kelly grasped my wrist and pulled me out of the kitchen and down the hall.

I frowned. "I told you. I'm not in the mood to go out."

"You've canceled on us for the past month."

I shrugged. "Busy."

"No more excuses. Tonight, we go out and get drunk."

"I have nothing to wear."

"Lies. We just went shopping." Kelly pushed my bedroom door open and stomped over to my closet.

I stretched out on the bed on my stomach with my hands under my chin, watching her ignore me. "As my friend, you should support my self-care."

She tossed two dresses on the bed and poked her head out. "Self-care with some dick!"

I burst into laughter. Kelly was seeing a new guy at her job and thought everybody needed a man like her. "Girl! What has that man done to you?"

Kelly turned with a jumpsuit in her hands.

"No, I don't have shoes to go with that."

She grabbed a pair of heels and held them against the jumpsuit. "Are you getting back in the saddle, or is someone else occupying your mind?" she asked, a hand planted on her hip.

"Nope. Single as a dollar bill."

Kelly picked out what she wanted me to wear and found the jewelry to match. Tugging me to my feet, she shoved everything into my arms and pointed me toward the bathroom to change.

* * *

An hour later, we made it to the club we'd frequented in the past. The music was so loud I could barely hear the guy in my ear trying to flirt. With his brown eyes and tall frame, he wasn't terrible looking, and his Gucci cologne smelled good. I dated all types of guys so long as they had personalities and treated me right. I'd let Kelly talk me into coming tonight, which somehow ended with her dancing with her boo. The bartender placed another tequila sunrise in front of me, and I thanked him with a generous tip.

"So, what do you think?" the guy asked, gesturing to himself.

"Huh?" I yelled, cupping my ear and leaning toward him. He wasn't taking the hint that I wanted to be alone.

"A date."

"A *mate?*" I scrunched my brows, offended by his comment. I wasn't the girl for breeding, even with my thick thighs and curvy hips.

He chuckled and closed the space between us. "Date. Tomorrow night."

"Um, well, I—"

"Shouldn't you be home figuring out how to do a better job on my ankle instead of entertaining this clown?"

The familiar and annoying voice grated on my nerves. I wanted to throw my drink in his face, but that would be a waste of a good drink.

"You're Destin Gray. The Tennessee Panthers starting kicker for the soccer team," the guy said excitedly. His adoration of Destin was embarrassing.

Destin might be famous, rich, and handsome, but he was a jerk. Cocky with a capital C. He smirked as I rolled my eyes. *How on earth did we end up at the same club?* Bad enough, we worked together.

"Is this you?" my so-called date asked Destin, pointing at me.

Destin grinned, slamming the drink on the counter. "Nah, she's all yours, man."

"Shit, she's fine as fuck, man. I'm planning on hitting that," the guy boasted.

I choked on my drink and turned to see Destin with a stern glare. I wasn't sure why he looked pissed. It wasn't as if we were friends or dating.

"Watch your mouth. Get the fuck on," Destin barked.

My eyebrows rose in surprise at his defense of me. All he did at work was piss me off.

"Sadie! Come dance with me, girl." Kelly came over and stretched her arm around my shoulder, bumping me with her hip.

"My fault, bro. Can I get your autograph?" the guy asked Destin.

My fist begged to be let loose. "Seriously?" It shouldn't have surprised me because women did the same thing around Destin.

The guy opened his mouth to respond, but I raised my hand to stop him. "Leave, please."

"Who is he?" Destin asked.

"None of your business," I hissed, grabbing Kelly's hand and walking away.

I figured I wouldn't see his face after leaving work, but everywhere I turned, he was there. I headed back to my car, dragging Kelly with me.

Kelly fanned herself as we climbed in. "Girl, that man is fine."

"Drink some water and calm down." I dropped the bottle in her lap and slipped the key into the ignition. "Ugh, please don't break down now."

"Told you to get it checked at the garage."

"Not now, Kelly."

"If not now, when? How about we get Destin to drop us off?"

"No."

"He's right there. You work together."

"So?"

"It's the perfect time to talk and get to know each other."

"I'd rather go back and ask the guy out that was in my face."

Our heads flew to the driver's window as someone tapped on it. I rolled it down to see Destin with his arms around two girls.

"You need help?"

"No."

"Yes," Kelly answered at the same time.

"I want to hear you say, 'I need help, Destin.'"

"Never."

"Do you know her?" the shorter woman with a blonde bob cut asked him.

"No," I snapped.

"Go to the car and wait," Destin instructed.

"But Destin—" she protested, running a hand over his chest and giggling as he smacked her ass.

I tried the car again, finally getting it to start. I turned back to Destin with a smirk. "You can go back to your little date."

He leaned in the window. "Jealous?"

I put the car in drive. "Nothing to be jealous of. Try not to give her the clap this time."

"I didn't take you for the type who believed everything on social media," he mumbled, moving away from the window.

I motioned for him to leave. "We're good here."

"You sound like a bitter woman who didn't get to leave with me." He blew me a kiss.

Flipping my hair, I left the parking lot, glancing in the rearview mirror to see him pressing the blonde against the car door.

Kelly laughed. "How wet did he get you?"

I turned on the radio. "I will never get wet for Destin Gray."

Chapter 3

Destin

I was still single at thirty-two, and my mother was always on my back about finding someone to marry and settle down with.

It became evident during the meeting with Coach, Elise, and the management team that my brush with the police was a bigger issue than I thought. I figured Coach was pissed off and at his wit's end.

"Destin, you're a top athlete, but you've slacked off when it comes to being a leader," he said.

"My job is to win championships," I argued.

"You're trending because you were caught in a compromising situation. That doesn't help us win games," Coach pointed out.

Simon, the majority owner of Tennessee Panthers, was listening to our exchange, along with my lawyers and Elise. I'd had interest from all the big leagues, but I signed with the Panthers because they wanted me as the leader and star. I wanted a place where I could grow and become the face of the franchise rather than riding under someone else. There was already jealousy within my team, plus outside rivals who thought my lucrative contract was ridiculous. Because of my performance over the last few months, Coach was talking about me not starting in games.

I shrugged. "I wasn't arrested, so what's the problem?"

"The problem is your image as a bad boy who doesn't care about his community or team."

"I never pretended to be some community hero."

"Destin," Elise warned, trying to calm me down.

"For real, Elise. They knew I wasn't a role model. We all knew it."

"We've come up with a plan to get things back under control and heal your ankle," Simon said, pushing a folder toward me.

Flipping it open, my gaze zoomed in on the phrase *agreement of marriage*. I burst into laughter. "Who's getting married?"

"You," Coach pointed at me.

I looked at Elise, whose expression remained neutral. I nudged the papers. "Did you know about this?"

She cleared her throat. "Just listen to what they're proposing."

"Playing games, Elise?" I stood, but Elise grasped my hand.

"Either you do this or look into a different field of play. The last few games, you've been off, and the doctors said you're not listening to them," she said, her eyes pleading.

Arthur, my lawyer, should have my back, but I knew even he was tired of my constant calls to bail me out.

I picked up the papers and read the documents. "Simon, you've lost your mind if you think I'm getting married."

"What do you propose?" Simon clasped his hands as he stared at me.

"Nothing. It will blow over. But I hear you about my health. I'll go back to physical therapy."

"We have a game this week, Destin. If we don't win, our chances of getting into the championship are slim," Coach said.

"The last time we won was four years ago, and you've become too much of a hothead to get out of your own way," Simon accused.

"I'm not getting married," I argued.

"Marriage would be good for your image, Destin," Elise said.

Going back and forth was pointless. "Who says, Elise? I'm not you and Sean."

Arthur finally spoke up. "My client needs time to review the information."

I wanted to knock him out for suggesting I would contemplate getting married.

"Public opinion brings in the money, and you're costing us too much," Simon stated.

"Like I said, I'll go to physical therapy." I dropped the papers on the table and strolled out of the room.

I headed to the field. I needed to get back into game mode and ignore everything else.

Bobby, the Panthers goalie, approached with the ball in his hand. He tossed it to me with a snicker. "Not a good meeting?"

"I need to work on my image."

Bobby's lips twisted in a smile. "Destin, we're boys, and I have my own dirt, but you trippin'."

"How? I'm young and single. I like to go out and have fun." I stretched my arms and legs, wincing as I pulled on my right ankle.

"Ankle still bothering you?"

"Yeah, man. Based on what the doctors say, I might have to sit the game out."

"Should have listened to them last time."

"And miss out on a game that could put us close to the big win?"

"Sometimes you have to put your health first, my boy." Bobby picked up his water bottle and took a sip.

"Let's run some plays real quick."

"Maybe finding a cute girl ain't bad."

"They're talking about marriage."

Bobby spit out the water. "Marriage!" He laughed like it was the most insane thing in the world. "I can't see you married with kids."

"That's what I said. They want me to sign an agreement."

Bobby scratched his head. "Negotiate. Tell them you'll date someone for a few months to help clean up your image like they do in Hollywood."

"My image is fine. You wanna go to a strip club?"

"You know I'm down." Bobby and I slapped hands, and he passed the ball to me to start practicing.

* * *

I stood in the back of the locker room after practice, watching Sadie's naive flirtation. I waited for her familiar giggle that drove me crazy. Seeing Oscar holding Sadie's hand while she checked his leg injury pissed me off. I was ready to break up their laughing fest and get him suspended. It was no secret that he was more of an arrogant hothead than Bobby and me.

We'd had a back-and-forth spat for the longest time. She'd called me an ass the other day, thinking I couldn't hear her. I'd wanted to go back at her, but Coach and I had been in the middle of a heated discussion. Being his daughter got her privileges in this business. The rest of us had to work hard to get where we were.

Sadie's five-six height only brought her up to my chest. She reminded me of the actress from True Blood with her warm brown eyes, flawless skin, and curls. I imagined tossing her over my shoulder and spanking her rounded ass for pissing me off. She had a smart mouth with me, but not when she was around her father or flirting with everyone else.

Sadie had started work here a year ago, and Simon and the higher-ups had liked her enough to keep her around. I could admit she was okay at her job, but the woman always thought she was right.

I'd put off the doctor's orders when I hurt my ankle months back, and after minor surgery, I avoided therapy and jumped right back into playing.

"Yo, Destin! What are you staring at?" Bobby pulled me from my thoughts as he poked me in the arm.

"Uh, nothing, man." I lifted my gym bag on my shoulder.

"Could fool some people, but not me, bro." His brow hiked in amusement.

I flipped him off, and he laughed.

"What's up, Sadie? You look extra sexy today," Bobby said, reaching for her hand and kissing her palm.

Sadie rolled her eyes and snatched her hand back.

"Bobby, watch yourself, boy," Coach Lester barked as he came up beside her.

Bobby spread his hands wide. "Coach, you know Sadie loves me."

"Sadie doesn't want a player with three outstanding DNA tests," Coach Lester joked.

Everybody in the locker room laughed as Bobby waved him off.

"She can speak for herself, and you're right, Coach," Sadie intervened. "Bobby, you need to work on protecting that little head before protecting the goal," she sassed, dropping her eyes to his groin.

The room erupted in laughter again.

"Sadie, forget Bobby. I need help with my ankle swelling up with this wrap," Oscar whined like a little bitch.

"Bullshit," I coughed.

Sadie whipped her head to face me. "Excuse me, Destin. Do you have something to say?" She braced her hand on her hip and glared at me.

"Maybe figure out how to wrap an ankle properly," I responded.

Sadie scoffed. "You know what—"

"You two cut it out." Coach Lester got between us, and the entire room went silent.

"The love birds need a time-out before they explode," Bobby teased.

I smacked him on the back of the head.

"Pigs will fly the day I fall in love with Destin," Sadie replied, turning her focus back to Oscar.

I closed the space between us. "What's that supposed to mean?"

Our eyes met, and her breathing hitched as something

like electricity passed between us. The only reaction she usually caused in me was annoyance, but right now, my shaft twitched under her intense gaze.

Bobby whistled and broke the spell. What the fuck was wrong with me?

Chapter 4

Sadie

I took after my father in my love of sports. He'd worked in different colleges for years as a coach in basketball and football, I fell in love with soccer while watching him eventually settling as head coach for the Panthers.

Most people thought a little girl should play with dolls and be cosseted and protected. Not me. My love of sports came from hanging out with my dad at games, learning the ins and outs of defense and offense, and being in a team. I thought it would make my father see me after finding out he and my mother couldn't have more kids, but he was too caught up in work and building his legacy. My mother understood the sadness in my heart because I wasn't the boy he'd always wanted. But I knew that Lester Myers loved me in his way.

Dad squared his posture in the chair. "Pass me the green beans, Sadie."

"Huh?"

"Where's your head, Sadie? I asked for the green beans," Dad repeated.

I grabbed the bowl and passed it to him. "Oh, sorry. Here you go."

"How was work today?" Mom asked.

"Fine."

"Except for being in Oscar's face," Dad mumbled, chewing on his ribs.

I sighed. "That's called doing my job."

"Don't you two start," Mom fussed.

"Tell your daughter to focus on the job at hand."

I dropped my fork and rubbed my forehead. My father and I arguing was a common occurrence at our family dinners. "Unbeknownst to you, Dad, I *have* been focused on making the lead physical therapist and saving up to start my own practice. Everyone on the team thinks I do a great job except you."

"Sadie, calm down," Mom urged.

"Show me a little respect, Sadie," Dad said. "You didn't just glide into the position on your own."

"Lester!" Mom shouted.

Tears pricked my eyes. I knew people thought I got the position because of my father, but it couldn't be further from the truth. I'd worked my ass off, pounding the pavement when it came to interviewing and putting in the time at various facilities to gain experience. I'd become hardened to hearing other people say it, but it cut me deeply when my own father wouldn't acknowledge my hard work.

"What? She needs to humble herself," he spat.

I jumped up and threw my napkin on the table. "Like you? You've gone from team to team because you over-played your hand," I accused.

"Sadie!" Mom gasped.

"Sit your grown ass down and stop running away." Dad pointed at the table.

"You two need to calm down before you say something you can't take back," Mom said, trying to be the neutral party.

I shook my head. "I'm not hungry anymore."

"Ungrateful," Dad muttered, sipping on his beer.

"Lester, I let you get away with a lot, but she's our baby girl, and you will show some respect."

"Mom, it's fine. I need to get started on some papers for an appointment tomorrow."

"Are you sure, Sadie?" Mom stood and came around the table to hug me.

"Yes, I have an early appointment," Checking the time on my watch.

"All right, baby. Call me tomorrow."

I kissed her on the cheek and grabbed my purse, swiping away a few stray tears as I left my childhood home. Climbing into my car, I slammed the door behind me. I closed my eyes and counted to ten, trying to calm myself, when my phone rang.

"Ugh, who is this?"

"Is that how you answer the phone?"

My eyes popped open at the sound of a deep rich voice.. I pulled the phone from my ear to see an unknown number on the screen.

"Who is this?" I turned up the volume to capture the name through the loud music in the background.

"I need you to meet me for a session tomorrow."

"Destin?"

"Yeah, big head."

I ended the call, started the car, and backed out of the driveway.

My phone rang again.

Shaking my head, I clicked to answer, pushing it through Bluetooth. "Hello."

"Did you hang up on me?"

"Destin?"

"Who the fuck else would it be?" he snapped.

"Boy, watch your mouth! I'm not your little ho. You don't dictate over here."

"Destin, who are you talking to?" someone asked in the background.

"Girl, go brush your teeth before you come into my space. Bobby, pass the bottle over here."

I stopped at a light. "I'm hanging up."

"You hang up on me again, and we're going to have problems," Destin warned.

I sped through the traffic, ignoring his little threats.

"Where are you?" he asked.

"None of your business."

"Yo, Bobby. Let's grab another bottle and some girls," he suggested.

"Man, we got a game tomorrow," Bobby chimed in.

I shook my head. "If you have an emergency, I advise you to call the police."

"Don't hang up on me."

His commanding voice somehow had me in a trance. "Are you drunk?"

"No. But I need you to be ready for a session tomorrow."

I ignored his demands. "Again, you need to go through the proper channels."

He chuckled. "Whatever, Sadie."

I shivered at the way he said my name.

"Sadie?"

I cleared my throat. "Yeah?"

I heard rustling over the phone. "This is Bobby. Can you do me a favor and come help with this crazy motherfucker, please?"

I leaned my head against the rest. "Bobby, that's not in my job description."

"I know, pretty lady, but he's drunk off his ass, and if something happens again, he might get kicked off the team."

"Who are you calling a pretty lady?" I heard Destin slur in the background.

Bobby cursed. "Get back, Destin."

Deep down, I didn't want anything to happen that put either of them in danger. I knew his reputation, and he needed to stop all the partying. Kelly always told me I was too nice. "Fine. Where are you?"

"Paris Night Out."

"The strip club?"

"Yeah, you've been here before?" Bobby questioned.

"A few times with some friends."

"What did she say?" Destin tried to get in on the conversation again.

"Luckily, I'm five minutes away." I turned at the lights near Summer Freeway and pulled into the shopping center.

"Come in for a second," Bobby said.

"Bobby—"

"Promise to drop a few bands in your hand."

"I'm not doing this for money." I turned the car off and climbed out, stomping toward the building where a crowd of men was waiting outside to enter.

"Hey, Sexy!" one of the men yelled.

I approached the doorman. "Excuse me. I'm meeting Bobby Coleman and Destin Gray inside."

"Straight to the back," the doorman replied.

I headed inside to see a bunch of girls twerking in front of Destin, who held two bottles. I marched over and tapped him on the shoulder.

"Bring me another bottle," Destin demanded, shoving one of the bottles into my hand.

"First off, I'm not the help. Second, it's time to go."

"Thanks for coming, Sadie. He's on one," Bobby said, appearing beside me.

I waved him off. I just wanted to get Destin home safe and in bed so I could forget this night had happened.

Destin's face screwed up as he looked at Bobby. "You called her."

"Somebody needs to help me get you out of here before folks start recording your dumb ass," Bobby defended, snatching the bottles from his hands.

"Ladies, he's done for the night," I announced to the twerking girls.

"Are you his wife or something?" A girl wearing a tiny thong and bra set with a garter belt planted a hand on her hip.

"Hell, no!" Destin and I answered at the same time.

"Then he's staying, right, Daddy?" she purred, rubbing Destin's chest.

Disgusted and ready for bed, I grabbed Destin's ear and pulled him out of the VIP section. The girls tried to come up behind us, but his security pushed them back.

"Girl, have you lost your mind?" Destin yanked away from me, but I grabbed his keys and dropped them in my pocket. "Give me my keys, or I'll take them back."

"Try, and I'll put you on your knees for touching me."

Destin frowned. "Who called you?"

"You did!" I slapped him on the back of the head.

"D, she's taking you home," Bobby chuckled, leaning in to hug me.

He poked his lip out like a big baby. "She ain't in charge of me."

"Boy, I swear you are running on my last nerve. Get in the car, please." I held the back door open.

"Why can't I ride in the front?" Destin challenged.

"Because I'd rather not look at your pathetic ass."

His phone rang, and he cursed under his breath. "Shit."

"Who's that?" Bobby asked.

"Elise." Destin blew out a breath and slid the phone back into his pocket.

"She probably found out you out here wildin' again," Bobby joked.

I started my car and pressed on the horn, causing them to jump.

"Quit playing." Destin reached in through the window and tried to take the keys.

I smacked the top of his head. "Get in or get left."

"Bro, get in the car before she leaves your dumb ass," Bobby said.

"Why can't you drive me home?" Destin asked.

"Got a nightcap." Bobby rubbed his hands together, indicating the two strippers standing by his car.

"Sucker." Destin laughed, and they fist-bumped before Bobby jogged to his car. Finally, Destin climbed into the passenger seat.

"Seat belt, please."

Destin scoffed. "You're bossy."

"Shut up." I hit the gas and sped out of the parking area, causing him to glare at me.

The car ride was silent for the next fifteen minutes.

"Where do you live?"

"Why?"

My night was getting longer and longer. I threw my hands up. "So I can drop you off?"

"Take the freeway to Germantown." He typed his address into the Satnav.

Sitting back in the seat, he texted on his phone, and I turned up the music. His place wasn't far from the club, but it was a thirty-minute drive for me. I lived in an apartment close to the city and wanted to save for a house one day. Maybe I could pick his brain when he sobered up tomorrow.

Arriving at his gated community, I watched as he typed something on his phone, and the doors opened, allowing me to drive up to the front entrance.

He looked at me as he ran a hand over his face.

"What?" I waited for the next insult.

"Thanks for bringing me home. I appreciate it."

"You're welcome."

The intensity of his stare did something to me that I hated because I couldn't stand his arrogant ass.

He cupped the back of my head, snaking his tongue into my mouth before biting on my top lip. It was all over before it began. Pulling back, he opened the door, stepped out of the car, and jogged into the house.

"Did that just happen?" I muttered to myself.

I touched my tingling lips as I left his property. I had no explanation for the kiss

"Get out of your head, Sadie."

Chapter 5

Destin

"Destin Gray leads up with the kick... and scores!" the announcer yelled.

I dropped to my knee, out of breath as I rubbed my ankle. "Shit." I hissed in pain.

Bobby jogged over. "Man, you good?"

I stood. "My ankle is giving me trouble."

Bobby stretched my arm over his shoulder and helped me to the locker room as the crowd in the stadium clapped.

"You're done for the last thirty minutes," Coach said.

"I'm all good Coach. Just need a minute," I pleaded my case.

"You're not good. Listen to me for once and take your ass in the back to see Sadie." Coach motioned for the locker room.

In no mood to argue, I stumbled into the back room to get patched up and back out on the field. "George, get out," I demanded, gesturing to the door.

"You can't kick me out," George challenged.

Bobby chuckled. I pick up his crutches and hold them up to take.

"What are you doing?" Sadie's arm wrapped around me, trying to snatch the crutches as I moved them behind my back. George cleared his throat.

I was ready to get back to the game. "I need you to check my ankle."

"Wait your turn," Sadie grumbled.

"We're in the middle of a game. I need to get back out there."

"She's working on me first," George muttered.

I snarled, tossing his crutches in the trash.

"Destin!" Sadie gasped.

Bobby got between George and me before I could knock him on his ass.

"Do it, and get locked up," George antagonized.

I balled up my fists. "Fuck you!"

"George, I'm sorry about this, but we'll reschedule for tomorrow," Sadie said, grabbing his crutches and positioning them under his arms.

"You lucky she's here." George bumped my shoulder as he passed.

I waved him off.

"If you want my help, I suggest you be quiet." Sadie folded her arms over her chest.

Last night, I made the mistake of kissing this woman. I blamed it on the alcohol because she wasn't my type. I couldn't stand a woman who tried to handle me unless it was my mom, Shelly, or Elise. I was used to them cursing me out, but Sadie should be falling in line like the other girls who swooned over me.

"He's going to behave. Right, D?" Bobby slapped my chest.

"Yes," I said through clenched teeth.

Sadie slipped on her gloves and tapped the table. "I take my job seriously, and you're getting checked, or I'm not releasing you to play."

I climbed on the table and propped myself up on my elbows. "You can't do that."

Sadie leaned forward. "Try me and see."

Bobby glanced between us. "Y'all might as well sleep together and get it over with."

"Get out!" Sadie and I said in unison.

Bobby held up his hands. "Seriously, Sadie, if he gives you any more problems, call me. Maybe she can help with your little problem, D."

"What problem?" Sadie asked, lifting my ankle.

I winced in pain. "Fuck! Focus on my ankle."

"It's a sprain. It'll heal with rest and time off," she announced.

I glowered at her. "I need to be back in the game."

Sadie shook her head. "Sorry, you're not going back out today."

"You're enjoying this, aren't you?" I asked through gritted teeth.

Sadie pulled off her gloves. "Enjoy you busting in my office for the second time and interrupting my session like you're the only one who needs my help? No, Destin, not enjoying it at all!" she shouted, getting in my face.

I had the urge to capture her lips, but this time I didn't have alcohol in my system. I ran my hand up her arm to the back of her head.

"Destin," Sadie moaned, causing my dick to harden. She gripped the front of my shirt.

"Sadie Myers!"

We jumped apart at the loud voice.

Sadie's cheeks flamed in embarrassment. "Coach, it's not—"

"Is this what you do to get ahead?" he demanded, stalking over to her.

"Hold on now, Coach." I hopped off the table and approached him. I felt bad for getting her into this situation.

"Destin, remember what I said. Lay off your ankle, and I expect to see you in a week," Sadie said, walking to her desk.

"While you two were back here locking lips, Oscar got the winning score," Coach bragged, stomping out of the room.

I moved to stand in front of Sadie's desk. "I'm sorry about that."

"It's fine," Sadie murmured, typing on her computer.

"Can you wrap my ankle before I go?"

"Shit! I forgot." Sadie jumped up and came around to help me back to the table.

"Hey, he didn't mean what he said."

Sadie smiled. "Doesn't matter. He only sees me as a mouth to feed."

"What do you mean?"

Sadie pulled out supplies to wrap my ankle. "Growing up with him as a father wasn't always rainbows and daddy-daughter dates."

"Sorry to hear that."

"Why did you kiss me?" she blurted.

"Nice change of subject."

"Habit."

The door flew open, and I turned to see Elise stroll in with a harsh glare. "I'd like to know the answer to that question."

"Elise, not now."

"Yes, now." Elise rubbed her pregnant belly as the players entered the locker room, celebrating our win.

Everybody was getting on my nerves. "Shouldn't you be with your husband?"

Elise raised an eyebrow. "Try again because I have another situation."

"I went to the strip club. What's the big deal?"

"The big deal is that you were caught kissing Sadie. It's trending all over social media." Elise shoved her phone in our faces.

"Oh, my god." Sadie took the phone from her hand.

"Yeah, and Simon wants to see you now," Elise added.

"I'll be there in a minute."

"Not just you. Sadie, too."

"Why?" We both asked.

"He thinks it could work out in your favor if you and Sadie fake date," Elise explained.

Sadie burst into laughter.

"What's funny?" I demanded.

"You and me in a relationship? That's crazy," Sadie replied.

Elise nodded. "At first, I thought the same thing, but your work situation makes it easy to convince the public you've fallen in love."

"I don't even like him, let alone love him." Sadie chuckled.

I grunted at her trying to play me off. "Girl, calm down. The feeling's mutual."

She waved me off. "You're the one who kissed me. Twice." She held up two fingers.

"Don't flatter yourself," I scoffed.

Elise tapped her foot impatiently. "Enough, Destin. We need to go talk with Simon."

I slid off the table and followed Elise down the hall, ready to get this conversation over with.

"You too, Sadie," Elise said.

I paused in my tracks. "Why is she coming?"

"Yeah. I've never had a problem with Simon," Sadie huffed.

"Sorry, girl. I tried," Elise responded.

A chill ran up my spine. Elise was keeping something from me.

We made it to Simon's office, and he waved us inside. He was smoking a cigar, surrounded by reporters taking pictures.

"Come in and take a seat." Simon's smile meant he had an idea I wouldn't like.

The reporters were escorted from the room, and I took a seat, sliding my hands into my pockets. "What's up, Simon?"

"Have you thought about our discussion the other day?"

"I'm not getting married."

"Married!" Sadie interrupted, reminding me she was in the room with us.

"Sadie, shouldn't you help get the players situated? I know a few need getting taped up," Coach said with a stony smile.

"Hold on, Lester. I requested her to be here," Simon pointed out.

An alarm went off in my head.

"For what?" Coach's eyes moved from Simon to Sadie and me before ballooning wide.

"Why am I here, Mr. Mclean?" Sadie asked.

"Please, call me Simon. You're here because I saw the photos of you and Destin."

"A private matter. I was drunk," I explained, not that it made the situation any better.

"Yes, well, you've had too many 'private matters' lately, and we think it's time you slowed down." Simon shot a glance at me from the corner of his eye.

"How slow?"

"Simon thinks it would be a good idea if you and Sadie start dating," Elise said.

Sadie laughed.

My stomach churned at her offense. "What's funny?"

Sadie giggled. "Are you hearing what they're saying?"

"It's not that funny."

"I want you two seen at events together to get things back on track. Charity functions, on social media, and magazine interviews," Simon announced, opening the desk drawer and sliding a file in front of us.

"No," Coach Lester snarled.

"I can speak for myself, and no is the answer, Mr. Mclean," Sadie said firmly.

"Sadie, you're in a great position as assistant therapist, but what if I could give you access to more clients? Perhaps an exclusive contract with the team for five years?" Simon asked, sweetening the pot.

"He's with a different girl every other day," Coach growled. "She'd be another notch on his belt."

I raised my hand. "I get a say in this, right?"

"No." Elise and Simon spoke at the same time.

"This contract stipulates you date for six months to a year, at the end of which you'll receive a bonus of a hundred thousand dollars, plus an extended contract with the Panthers," Simon stated.

"Sadie, you're not taking the deal. I forbid it." Coach pointed his finger in her face.

"The kiss was nothing," I said. "No reason for me to get a hired girlfriend."

"The blogs and news are reporting you're frequenting strip clubs and playing house with the team therapist," Elise said.

I rubbed a hand over my face. I knew the shit was bad. "I can't find someone else to pretend to be my girl?"

"No, it has to be Sadie," Simon said.

"Why? We hate each other."

"He's right," Sadie agreed.

Simon smirked. "Besides Elise, she's the only one who doesn't put up with your shit."

I narrowed my gaze on him. "Six months, and you'll leave me alone?"

Simon held my gaze. "Six months to a year, and I decide at the end if you continue as the star player."

"Wait, you're pulling me from the roster?"

"For now. You need to focus on your health. Oscar is the star forward in the meantime."

"Simon, you know that's bullshit!" I exploded.

"Until you show me differently, I'm putting him in the next game for the cup," Simon said resolutely.

Elise started typing on her phone, which meant shit was already out in the media about me being replaced.

"I haven't agreed to anything," Sadie pointed out.

"All right, I'll sign the damn contract." Picking up the pen, I signed and dated my full name on the line.

Simon grinned, and I felt like a bitch letting him dictate my life.

"Sadie, I know you have a private life, but it would

mean a lot to the team. This is about your and Destin's careers in the long run," Elise insisted.

Simon held out the pen I used to sign, and Coach Lester stood back, shaking his head. Sadie looked between her father, me, and Simon. Seconds ticked past before she finally took the pen and signed her name.

Chapter 6

Sadie

I was meeting Kelly and Elise for lunch because Elise was setting up a magazine interview. A month had passed, and Destin and I still hadn't been on a fake date, although he was in the media for other things.

Simon had made the deal even sweeter, enticing me with my own clinic if the Panthers made it to the World Cup. Destin's foot seemed to be better, judging by the photos of him dancing with girls in various clubs.

Tossing the phone on the table, I waved at Kelly as she approached the table. I stood to hug her, pulling her chair out as she removed her jacket.

"I'm starving. Have you ordered?" Kelly asked.

"No, I was waiting for you and Elise."

Kelly picked up the menu. "Is she on her way?"

Checking the time on my phone, I nodded. "Here she comes now." I smiled at Elise's husband walking behind her like security. He was the star player, but in Elise's eyes, he was the grand prize.

"Hi, Elise. Sean." I hugged them, noticing Sean was wearing his practice clothes.

"Hey, Sadie. Sorry I'm late. This one wanted to sleep in a little longer." Elise rolled her eyes at him.

"Baby, stop lying. You know you wouldn't let me leave the bed," Sean teased.

I chuckled at their banter.

"Please go somewhere, Sean. Call me after practice." Elise grabbed his chin and kissed him on the lips.

Sean gently pulled on her ponytail. "See how she treats me, Sadie?"

A soft smile rose on her face. I loved seeing beautiful love like theirs. Dating hadn't been my focus, but I wanted to get back out there once I finished this deal for Destin.

"Elise, this is my best friend, Kelly." Kelly extended her hand to Elise.

"I'm starving," Elise said.

I waved the waitress to our table. "Me too," I grumbled, scanning the menu.

"Hi, ladies. I'll be your server today. My name's Coco."

I smiled at Coco. "Can I get shrimp tacos and a side of red rice?"

"That sounds good. I'll have the same," Kelly said.

"Can I get the steak tacos?" Elise asked.

Coco wrote down our orders. "Coming right up. Anything to drink besides water?"

"Pink lemonade," Kelly replied.

Elise scooted closer to the table. "Sadie, I can't thank you enough for doing this for Destin, even if *he* hasn't thanked you," Elise said, shaking her head.

"You ride for him more than he deserves, Elise," I replied.

She sighed. "He's like a brother to me. He gave me a

shot as a publicist before anyone else. Plus, he's best friends with Sean. Destin can be an asshole, but there's more to him than he allows most people to see, and I can't say he's not protective."

"He needs to get his life figured out," I sighed.

We talked until our waitress arrived with our food twenty minutes later. My stomach rumbled as she placed our orders in front of us.

"The contract states you go on a few dates, be seen together, and do a few interviews," Elise said, putting sour cream on her tacos.

"No sex," Kelly blurted.

I choked on my drink. "Kelly, it's a business arrangement, nothing more. I'm not having sex with that man."

"Destin is fine. What's wrong with getting your back blown out a few times?" Kelly teased.

I wiped my mouth with the napkin. "You know me better than anyone. I am not a one-night stand girl, and Destin's not my type."

"What about that kiss?" Elise waggled her eyebrows.

"That was a mistake."

"Mistake?"

I whipped around at Destin's voice.

"What are you doing back here?" Elise asked as Sean took a taco off her plate, and Destin sat in the chair next to me.

"My boy wanted to talk to you, and I told him you were here," Sean said.

"Well, he could make an appointment for us to discuss business," Elise countered, smacking Destin's hand as he tried to take a taco.

"He's cute, Sadie," Kelly said, reaching out to shake Destin's hand.

Destin's smile was charming as he held her hand. "How you doing, beautiful?"

I removed Kelly's hand from Destin's. "Put the Casanova charm away for one second."

Destin lifted Kelly's hand again, his gaze taunting as he kissed her knuckles. "Jealous?"

"Destin, act like you have some sense. We need to talk about a few events I planned for you and Sadie." Elise said.

Destin turned to me. "My ankle is finally back to normal. You were right about taking it easy."

His compliment made me feel good. I smirked. "Told you."

Elise pulled up her calendar on her phone. "Destin, I want you to be ready for a charity event for kids, and Sadie's going to be your date."

"Can't you write a check or something?" Destin grabbed my drink and took a sip.

"The waitress will gladly take your order," I sassed.

"Not hungry." Destin wiped his hands on the napkin and stood.

"The event will be good publicity, Destin. I expect you there with bells on," Elise said.

"When is it?" he asked.

"Tomorrow," Elise replied.

I groaned. "Elise, I have work."

"Simon's told the team that the assistant will handle your appointments," Elise explained.

Destin playfully mussed Elise's hair. "Sean, get your wife. She's killing my lifestyle."

"Playboy days are over, son," Sean replied, and Elise chuckled.

"What exactly is this event?" I asked.

Elise smiled. "Gifting toys to kids, and Destin is donating a generous check."

"I had a date at the Boom Boom Room," Destin complained.

"Boy!" Kelly cackled, sliding down her chair in laughter.

His pout made me laugh, too. "I'll meet you there."

"He'll pick you up, Sadie," Elise said firmly, winking at him.

"I don't mind driving, Elise," I said.

"No matter what they say on the streets, I am a gentleman. I'll pick you up," Destin said, reaching into his pocket for his wallet.

I arched an eyebrow. "What are you doing?"

"Paying for your lunch, pretty lady."

"I can pay for my own lunch."

"No, she can't." Kelly shoved my arm, and Destin chuckled at our tussle.

"See? You're already making better decisions," Elise teased Destin.

Sean kissed her, and he and Destin left the restaurant.

"How is your family handling the situation?" Kelly asked.

"My dad is still pissed, but Mom is fine so long as he's respectful."

Elise patted my hand. "He'll come around, I promise."

* * *

The next day, I washed and conditioned my hair and put on full makeup. I wore a cute short set and Nike shoes since we'd be around kids in a gym.

Today was important to the community where Destin grew up. Even though he'd made that comment about just writing a check, Elise said he loved kids and giving back. I'd researched his background last night and scrolled through his social media. There were a lot of comments from girls wanting to hook up, but it was also evident that he showed a lot of love to his hometown of Binghamton.

Kelly was coming to support us, and Elise had invited a few reporters and photographers along with his teammates. Even Simon and his kids were coming, and my father had insisted on showing his face. Simon said it was a good photo opportunity for the team to show their support.

Destin stepped off the elevator as I closed and locked my apartment door.

"I told you I would meet you downstairs," I complained.

"Already paparazzi downstairs. It looks better if we leave together."

He reached toward me, and I eyed him suspiciously.

"Why are you looking like that?" he asked.

"You're being nice to me."

He laughed. "I was going to take your bag and escort you to the car. Is that acceptable?"

"Oh, okay." I let him take it for me.

"I can be a gentleman." Destin gestured to the elevator.

"Maybe that side of you is for the cameras only." I gazed at him thoughtfully. "You make it hard to hate you forever."

"Thanks, I guess."

We took the elevator down, and I pushed the door open. Destin grabbed my hand, and I smiled and waved as the cameras flashed. Destin ignored the barrage of questions and led me to the Escalade, opening the back door for me to climb inside.

"Do you have a driver every day?" I asked, making conversation as Destin slid in next to me.

Destin signed a few autographs before rolling up his window. "Sometimes, unless I want privacy."

"Where's the charity event?"

"Old high school. East High."

"You were a Mustang?"

He turned to face me. "What do you know about the Mustangs?"

"A few friends went to East High."

"Yeah, my old stomping ground until my parents got better-paying jobs and moved me to Germantown."

"What do your parents do?"

"My mom's a retired teacher."

"And your dad?"

He glanced at me. "A retired city construction worker."

"Wow, that's amazing."

"Yeah. What about your mom? I know Coach Lester, obviously," he said with a smirk.

"My mom was a postal worker." I sat back in the seat as the car pulled into the parking lot at the rear of the high school. Banners and balloons hung around trees, with Destin's name up top.

Destin peeked through my window. "Elise got every-body out here."

My gaze fell on his lips before wandering back to his eyes.

"What are you staring at, Sadie?"

"Huh?"

"You keep staring at me like that, and I'll start thinking you like me," he said with an arrogant grin.

"There you go, getting a big head."

"Me? Never." Shoving the door open, he clasped my hand in his. "I never let a lady open a door in my presence."

"You're like Mr. Jekyll and Mr. Hyde."

"How so?"

"One minute, you're doing nice things like carrying my bags and opening doors. The next, you're trying to boss me around."

"What can I say? I'm a complicated man," he sighed.

Destin stepped out and shook hands with reporters and directors on his way to my side of the car, where he opened the door to help me out.

Elise appeared next to me. "Stay close to me," she whispered in my ear.

I looked around. "I didn't expect this many people." The street was blocked off around the block.

"Destin's name commands attention." Elise grabbed some staff to escort us to the red carpet.

Destin frowned. "How many members of the press did you invite, Elise?"

"Enough that you're getting an interview with Vogue magazine." Elise clapped her hands in excitement.

"Damn. Vogue, huh?"

"I know, very major. So act right, please." Elise fixed on a smile and turned us to face the lineup of reporters.

"Destin Gray, tell us about today." Channel Seven

asked the first question.

"I'm here to support my people. You know I love to give back," Destin said smoothly.

"Who's the beautiful lady on your arm today?"

Destin held on tight to my hand. "Meet my girlfriend, Sadie Myers."

Elise moved us along the red carpet to a group of kids waiting to take pictures and get signatures from Destin. "We'll get a few pictures alone of Destin and then with you," she said.

"This is all about him. I can go inside and help set it up," I suggested.

"No. This works by showing you both off." Elise motioned for some kids to stand in front of us.

My smile widened at a few girls wearing Destin's jersey number and t-shirts. He high-fived them and crouched down to pose for photos with them.

"Are you getting good grades, Alecia?" Destin asked one of the girls.

"Yes, sir." Alecia grinned, and my heart fluttered at her cuteness.

"Call me Destin or D, Alicia. Only my favorite people get to call me by those names." He winked at her.

"You're pretty," Alecia said to me.

I tugged on the end of her pigtail. "Thank you, and you're gorgeous, Miss Alecia."

"Where are your parents, Alecia?" Destin asked.

"Inside, D." Alecia was already familiar with Destin and grabbed his hand.

"You've got competition already," Kelly joked.

I smiled as the little five-year-old held out her arms for him to pick her up. "She might be the only one to get him to be nice." Destin caught me staring and winked.

"Nope, that's all you and those sweet lips," Kelly teased, bumping my hip.

Elise picked up a few bags for us to start filling them up to give out. The basketball court was filled with different sections where parents could walk alongside to pick up one toy from various companies.

Destin laughed and joked with Alecia and her parents, and a few players took pictures with the parents as the DJ started the music. An hour later, Destin took the mic and got on stage to give a speech that had the audience laughing and cheering.

"So, all that remains is for me to thank my brothers on the field and the Tennessee Panthers for supporting my hometown." Destin finished to a rousing round of applause as he shook hands with the organizer.

"What do you think of Kids in Step?" he asked, coming to join me.

"I think you're doing something good here."

"Thanks. I appreciate you agreeing to do this. I know I haven't always been the easiest person to get along with."

"No, you don't say," I teased in mock horror.

He folded his arms over his broad chest. "I've given you a hard time."

"Hard time? Or trying to cause chaos?" I tapped a finger on my chin.

"Go to dinner with me."

Before I could answer, a group of kids ran over, pulling Destin toward the basketball machine. Having him ask me out on a real date was surprising and something I needed to think about because sex was not part of our agreement.

Chapter 7

Destin

Days later

"That's one up!" I yelled to Bobby as he dribbled the ball down the court in my basement.

I'd called the boys to hang out before meeting Sadie for dinner. It was two on two with Sean and Adam against Bobby and me. Most of my friends were players on the team, and I kept in contact with a couple of guys from my old stomping ground.

"Time-out," Adam said, pulling off his shirt and using it to wipe his face.

"You need to cover that bird's chest," I taunted.

"Fuck you, Destin. Sadie loves it." Adam kissed his right bicep, and the three of them laughed at my jealousy.

"Sadie finally agreed to go out with you?" Sean asked, pulling a bottle of water from his bag.

"Yeah."

Adam smirked. "Have you smashed yet?"

I glared at him. "Don't talk about her like that."

"He's officially in love," Adam announced, holding his hand out to Bobby and Sean as they handed him money.

"You three motherfucker's bet on me?"

"Hell, yeah." Adam laughed.

"Fuck y'all. Ain't nobody in love. She's cool," I said, running the ball through my legs.

"More than cool by the way you kept eyes on her at your charity a few days ago and in the locker room," Bobby recalled.

"Who's friend are you exactly?"

"I go where the money is," Bobby teased.

"Can't even count on my boys," I huffed.

"Have you talked with your parents?" Bobby asked.

"Not yet. I plan on introducing her to them."

Sean grabbed the ball from my hand and did a free throw. "At least you didn't have to get married."

"Hell, no. After six months, I'm back doing me." I licked my lips, thinking of all the pussy I was ready to fall into.

"So Sadie's up for grabs after six months?" Adam asked.

Adam pushing up on Sadie shouldn't bother me much, but we'd had great conversations lately, and I considered her a friend.

"Destin, how do you not know how to play Spades?" *Sadie joked over the phone.*

"What are you trying to say? All black people should know how to play Spades?"

She cackled in the background. "As the so-called bad boy, I expected more from you."

"Girl, I'm everything and the whole package."

"Do women really fall for that?"

"The truth?"

"You and your truth better strap up before you're on some talk show with five baby mommas and seven kids."

"No baby momma's over here."

"That's what your mouth says."

"What does your mouth say?"

The phone went silent.

"Cat got your tongue?"

"I need to get back to my patient."

"Who?"

"None of your business."

"If it's Oscar or George, I'm kicking their ass."

"This is my job, Destin."

"So?"

"Stop pouting," Sadie giggled.

"Have a good day, Sadie."

"You too, Destin."

"See? He's already daydreaming about the girl." Sean said, pulling me from my thoughts.

"Come on. I'm gonna beat your ass in this game and get my five hundred." I snatched the ball from Sean.

"Now we're talking." Adam rubbed his hands together.

Two hours later, I emerged from the shower. I dried off, grabbed a pair of boxers, and tossed the towel into the hamper.

Playing ball like old times made me homesick and want to hang out with my parents. Taking my phone off the charger, I dialed them up as I walked into my closet.

"Baby boy!"

Perry Gray was the only man I feared and respected on this planet. He raised me to be myself and not a shadow of what he wanted me to be. Being a black man in soccer came with a lot of judgment because most thought tall black men should stick to basketball or football, and I could play all three. I loved the rawness and adrenaline of competition. Like all professional sports, there was the risk of being injured, but I've liked the teamwork of the soccer world since I was a little kid.

"How are you doing, old man?"

"Take that 'old man' shit somewhere else."

Laughing, I tucked the phone between my shoulder and ear to slide on my watch and apply cologne.

"Where's Ma?"

"Next to me, where else?" he sassed.

"Why do you act like you got game, man?"

"Because I do, and your momma loves it."

"Perry!"

The loud shriek in the background had me tearing up in laughter. "Hey, Momma."

My Parents lived in the same house I grew up in, but eventually let me buy them a place near me.

"Hey, baby."

"Calling to check on y'all."

"We're good. We saw your charity function. Who's the girlfriend?"

"Carlene, leave the boy alone."

"I need to know if she's money hungry."

Mom was always calling to tell me what I needed to look out for with women and to keep my pecker in my pants.

"Ma, that's the agreement I told you about."

I hadn't kept anything from my parents, but they hadn't met Sadie yet, so it was only right Mom would question the pictures.

"Well, bring her home," Mom urged.

"Mom, this ain't a real thing."

"I'll be the judge of that," she replied.

"Get your wife, Pop."

"He can't *get* me," Mom scoffed.

Seconds later, I heard moaning. "Y'all too old for that," I said in disgust.

"Shit, you better catch up, son, because your father puts it down," he boasted.

That was my cue to say goodbye and end the call.

I headed downstairs to see Shelly dusting the ornaments and watching her soap operas.

"Shelly, those shows are going to rot your brain." I pinched her cheek as I passed, plucking my keys from the bowl on the hall table.

She frowned. "Hush. They may bring back my favorite character on Days of Our Lives."

"I'm heading out for the day."

"Okay." She waved as I left.

I slid into the Hummer, revved the engine, and backed out of the garage. I turned the music up, listening to Illmatic by Nas. I wanted to check in on Sadie. I hoped she wasn't entertaining another dude, or we'd have problems.

Arthur had looked over the agreement to ensure it was official. Although I'd signed it, he was good enough to get me out of contracts under any stipulation, which was why I paid his ass so much money.

Parking out in front of her building, I slipped out of the car and tossed the keys to the valet to move it from the no-parking zone. He recognized me, and the look of wonder on his face told me my car would be in the right spot when I came back down.

I took the elevator and knocked at Apartment Ten, slipping my hands into my pockets.

"Destin?" Sadie's expression was surprised as she answered the door.

"Pretty lady,"

"What are you doing here?"

"Who's at the door, girl?" Kelly, her best friend, approached from behind.

"Kelly, right?"

"Hey, Destin. What brings you here?" Kelly asked.

"Came to ask Sadie out for dinner."

Sadie frowned. "Do we have plans? Elise didn't email me."

"No plans. I'm here on my own."

"I like you." Kelly grinned, pulling the door open further.

Sadie stepped aside. "Sorry. Do you want to come inside?"

Nodding, I stepped into her place, gazing at the artwork on the wall. Her style was all her—simple, earthy tones.

"Sadie, call me later. I know you'll have plenty to talk about." Kelly waved goodbye.

Sadie rushed to stop her from leaving. "Kelly!"

"Do you bite, Destin? Or have any weird fetishes? I mean, I like some things, but...Ouch! Sorry, Sadie." Kelly's laughter followed her as she left the apartment.

Chuckling, I relaxed on her couch.

"Where do you want to go?" Sadie asked, turning back to me.

"A nice dinner. Nothing crazy. We need to be seen out together."

"Fine. Is this okay? I just got home from work an hour ago." Sadie motioned to her black slacks and the red top that showed off her plump breasts.

I nodded. "You look beautiful."

Sadie grabbed her keys and purse, and I helped her into her jacket.

"The enemy has manners," she teased.

"Tried to tell you."

"After you, Mr. Gray." Sadie held the door open for me to leave first and locked it behind us. I waited and took her hand as we walked out of the building.

"Keep holding my hand, and people will think we're a real couple."

"That's the point."

"Right."

Thirty minutes later, we made it to the Terrier, a Mexican restaurant I frequented when I wanted to be left alone. I walked Sadie through the door, and the music of the live mariachi band greeted us. Jose had known me for a long time and had reserved the same booth where I always ate in the back.

Sadie looked at me in surprise. "We're eating here?"

"Yeah, why not?"

"Doesn't seem like the type of place you would be seen at."

"What type am I?"

Sadie shrugged. "You like to party. This place is low-key."

Charlotte, our server, arrived at our booth with margaritas for Sadie and me before I could reply. "Hi, Destin."

"You ordered already?" Sadie asked.

"Yes. Is that okay? I come here a lot." The staff knew my order, and I'd doubled up for Sadie.

Sadie lifted the drink to her lips. "How did you know I would agree to dinner?"

I smirked. "Lucky guess."

"Very lucky."

"Charlotte, this is Sadie, my date. Treat her right."

Sadie snorted. "Funny."

"What's funny?"

Charlotte chuckled and shook her head as she left us to it.

"You told Charlotte to treat me right, yet you barely treat me with respect."

I wanted to clear the air between us since we would be in each other's lives for the next few months. "True, and I apologize."

Sadie frowned. "Why?"

"Why?"

"Yes. I never did anything to you."

"Honestly. I thought you were one of those girls who got a come-up from her family name. I had to work non-stop to get a chance at a scholarship." My family worked hard, but there was no money for college.

"Everything isn't what it seems, Destin. I was never given any favoritism as Lester Myers's daughter."

"Are you serious?"

"Yes. Sometimes I think my father hates me."

"Come on now, Sadie."

"I'm telling you the truth. He's always wanted to control my life."

"How did you get the job with the Panthers?"

"Busting my ass in school and getting a scholarship. At first, he wouldn't help me with college, but Mom finally got him to send some money each month. He's always said, 'You need to work like I did to make a name for yourself.'" Sadie mimicked her father's voice.

"Sorry to hear that."

Charlotte returned with our trays of tacos, queso, beans, and Mexican pizzas.

"Food looks good."

I smiled. "My favorite place to be alone."

"How is it to be Destin Gray?"

"Not all fun and games." I grabbed my fork and dug into the beans and tacos.

Sadie scooped a chip in the salsa and popped it into her mouth. "Having everything at your fingertips?"

"I can admit I became bullheaded and full of myself."

She covered her chest with her palm, pretending to be shocked. "No!"

I laughed. "You hating on me?"

"No. You're a jerk, Destin, and you need to realize that the world doesn't revolve around you. Plus, your choices and all those girls will end your career."

"Which girl should I be looking at?"

"Not a girl. You need a woman."

I ran my thumb over her chin to clean off a spot of sour cream. "Woman like you?"

"When's the last time you dated a plus-size woman?"

"What are you talking about?"

"I've never seen you with a woman with curves and love handles."

"You think I have a type?"

"All athletes have types with the BBL, large breasts, and fake teeth."

Chapter 8

Destin

Two months later, Sadie and I had been on multiple outings and were seen at different charity events as a couple. Something in me needed her validation that I wasn't like the image she had of all athletes.

Feeling confident about being back in the game, I waited for the next question from the magazine reporter.

"The Tennessee Panthers made it to the playoffs. How do you feel about that, Destin?"

The lighting was adjusted to get another shot of me standing with a soccer ball in my hand. "I feel great."

"As the team leader, you set the bar for the players' behavior on and off the field. Do you think you've been fairly judged?"

"Honestly, I know I got it wrong a few times, and I apologized to my team."

"Social media went crazy when you introduced Sadie Myers, a physical therapist with the Panthers. How does that work for you two?"

"Sadie can probably answer that better than me." I drew her in close, tucking her under my arm.

"Destin is very professional at work," Sadie commented.

"She whipped me into shape and got me back on the field," I said, looking down at her.

Elise gave us a thumbs-up from behind the camera.

"How long have you two been together?" the reporter asked.

Sadie smiled. "A few months."

"Rumor has it that this was all manufactured to fix your image. How do you answer that, Destin?"

Elise started to interrupt, and I held up a hand. "I'm the only one who could clean up my image, but Sadie helped to calm me down and focus on what was important—winning games and giving back to my community."

"Does your father, Coach Lester Myers, agree with you dating the star player?" The reporter directed the question to Sadie.

"As his only daughter, my father doesn't like me dating anyone," Sadie chuckled.

The reporter laughed. "Well, the World Cup is coming up, Destin, and your fans are hoping you can pull it off again."

"We're bringing it back home," I promised.

The reporter thanked us, and we took a few photos before Sadie went to change clothes.

I stood at the door and waited. "Are you still down for dinner with my parents?"

Sadie poked her head out of the changing room. "Do you think it's necessary? We only have a few more months before this is over."

Her answer gave me pause. I wanted more time and

needed to show her I was in this for real. I slid into the changing room to see her wearing a large t-shirt dress that showcased her soft curves.

Sadie placed her hand on her hip. "What are you doing?"

I tucked a piece of her behind her ear. "I'm doing this for real, Sadie. I'm not pretending."

"Since when?"

"Spending all this time together has had me rethinking my life choices."

"I'm not a rebound, Destin. I have real feelings and thoughts."

I grasped her hips, tugging her closer so she could feel my hardness. "You feel that?"

"Yes," she whispered.

"I'm not gonna lie. I've dated every type of woman. The blogs keep regurgitating the photos for clicks. So, there's no rebound. *You* do that to me." I leaned forward and kissed her forehead.

Her eyes found mine, and she studied me carefully for a minute. "Okay."

* * *

After dinner, I took Sadie to my place for a nightcap and to talk about our next steps with the contract. To have my parents tell me how much they liked her put a smile on my face. It showed me that not having her father on board didn't matter. So long as Sadie agreed to be my girl, I was all in for throwing the contract away.

Turning on the kitchen light, I reached for the bottle of wine Shelly set aside for me and took Sadie by the hand, leading her to the living room.

"Destin, your home is beautiful," she said, casting her eyes around.

"Mostly decorated by Elise and my mom."

"You rely on Elise a lot."

"My mom and Elise keep me level-headed."

"Your dad is funny."

"He needs to focus on his wife and not flirt with my date," I said dryly, popping the bottle open and pouring a small amount into a glass.

We sat on the couch, and I lifted the remote to turn on the music. Whitney Houston's Bodyguard soundtrack filtered into the room.

"Tell me what you're thinking?" I placed my glass on the table and lifted Sadie's legs onto my lap. Removing her heels, I massaged her feet.

Sadie rested her head on the couch and closed her eyes, moaning as I kneaded her tight muscles. "I'm thinking you must have superpowers to know that rubbing my feet puts me in a good mood." She opened her drowsy eyes and took a sip of her wine.

I plucked the glass from her hand, placing it on the table next to mine. Cupping her chin to tilt her face, I leaned in and kissed her. "I guess I have the magic touch."

"Is that what you think?"

"No. Kelly told me," I laughed.

Sadie swatted me on the chest. "She told you that?"

"Hell, no." I grinned.

Sadie drew in a breath. "I like you, Destin."

"Me, too."

"No, I mean, I like you for real. I've tried to fight these feelings and keep it strictly business, but my heart won't listen to my head."

"Then I'm a lucky man because I know how I came

across in the beginning. But you're not alone in these feelings, Sadie."

She pressed her forehead against mine and grasped the back of my neck. She sucked on my top lip and slid her tongue inside my mouth to dance with mine. I skimmed my hand down her side, gripping her thigh as our kiss became aggressive, almost animalistic.

"Destin," Sadie moaned.

Moving my hand in between us, I unbuttoned her pants, circling the elastic of her panties. Sadie lifted her hips in a blatant invitation, grabbing my wrist as I slipped my fingers between her wet folds.

"Let it go for me, baby."

"Destin!" She moaned my name louder this time.

I quickly removed her pants and threw them aside. Spreading her legs, I kissed my way up her inner thigh, peppering kisses along her stomach. She allowed me to drink my fill of her without hesitation. I loved a confident woman, no matter her size.

Delving my fingers into her hair, I tipped her head back to look me in the eye. "You're beautiful, Sadie."

"Take off your clothes," she huffed.

I snatched off my shirt and pants, tossing them aside and reclaiming her lips. Her arms wove around my neck as she lifted her hips, grinding against me and unleashing an unrelenting passion.

"Fuck, you're sweet, baby."

I watched her spit in her hand and wrap it around my dick, stroking up and down. Throwing my head back, I tried to hold my composure.

"Sadie," I grunted.

"Yes?" she whispered.

"I'm about to fuck you, baby."

"Do it."

She angled my dick to her opening, and I buried myself inside her tight pussy.

I plunged deep and pulled back, stroking a few more times as we caught our rhythm. "Ugh. Fuck, beautiful."

"Oh, god, Destin!"

I dropped my hands to her thighs, spreading them wider as I sank deep. Sadie pinched her nipples, and the sight drove me crazy. I pumped harder and faster, dipping my head to capture a nipple in my mouth and biting down gently. Our bodies collided, rocking the couch.

Sadie moaned and arched her back, her breathing ragged.

"Destin, keep going. I'm almost there."

"Yeah, you ready to come?"

I slipped my hand between us, finding her clit and circling it with my thumb, watching as her luscious body came undone.

"I'm coming!" she moaned.

"That's right, beautiful. Come for me, baby." My hips pistoned as I slammed into her, and my orgasm washed over me.

"Damn, Sadie," I said once I caught my breath. I smoothed my hand over her back, gazing into her eyes.

She sighed. "Yeah."

But our passion was far from sated. We went another round, this time on the floor, followed by the shower. Then we fell into bed and slept.

Chapter 9

Sadie

Weeks later

Destin waved to the fans and walked toward me after signing a few autographs. If anyone had told me a few months ago that I would be the girlfriend of one of the highest-paid soccer players in the country, I would've laughed in their faces.

We were on our way to dinner with my parents, followed by a weekend getaway with Elise and Sean for a couple's trip at a cabin.

"Are you sure about going to dinner with my parents?" I asked worriedly.

"It won't be that bad."

"This is Lester Myers we're talking about."

Destin brushed his lips against mine. I gripped his shirt and deepened the kiss briefly before reluctantly pulling back.

Destin kissed my knuckles. "Your father and I have an understanding,"

"What kind of understanding?"

"One of mutual respect."

My brow hiked up. "Sounds like I should worry."

"Nope. He's cool, and so am I."

"Where's security?" I asked, glancing back at the stadium as we climbed into the car.

"In the blacked-out SUVs."

Destin started the car and drove out of the reserved spaces to get on the road.

I was counting down the days for us to be alone again after our first time having sex. He was the biggest I'd ever experienced. Everything they said about men with big feet having big dicks was true. I smiled as I remembered running away from his huge dick only to be caught and fucked to within an inch of my life. I got my revenge by using my mouth and tongue on him until he begged for mercy.

Destin eyed me suspiciously. "What are you grinning about?"

"Just thinking about getting you alone again."

He grinned at me as we pulled up outside my parent's house.

The TV was blaring as I walked inside with Destin. We headed down the hallway and into the living room to see my father watching a recap of the game.

"Hey, Dad."

He turned and tipped his chin at us.

"Destin, this is my father, Lester Myers," I introduced formally.

"Coach, you know we had it all along, right?" Destin said, indicating the game. He released my hand and walked further into the living room.

"You almost lost your footing on the last one," Dad grunted, pausing the TV.

"Great. Sports talk," I sighed. "I'll leave you men to it." I left the room and went to find Mom.

"Hi, sugar," she greeted me when I found her in the kitchen. She held her arms out for a hug.

"Hey, Mom."

"What's wrong?" she asked hearing my lackluster tone.

"Dad is talking sports with Destin," I said, stealing a chunk of carrot from the steamer.

"Is that bad?"

"Yes, because he's going to ignore everything else."

"Sadie, stop worrying. Your dad loves you and is proud of you." Mom passed me the plate of lamb chops.

"He said that?"

"Lester never has to say it. But I talked to him, and I think he'll surprise you."

I put the plate on the table and raised my hand to her forehead.

"What are you doing?"

"Checking you're not sick."

Mom chuckled and went to get the steamed vegetables.

Ten minutes later, we all said grace and started to eat as a family.

"So, Destin. Sadie told me you're taking her out of town," Mom said.

"Yes, ma'am."

Mom beamed, putting some lamb chops onto his plate. "You sure are wooing our baby."

Destin looked at me. "She's special and keeps me on my toes."

"That's my girl," Mom said proudly.

Dad cleared his throat, and I waited on pins to hear what he'd say. He wiped his mouth and placed the fork down, clasping his hands on the table. "Sadie is our only child, and although I've been hard on her, she means the world to her mother and me."

"Dad—"

"Let me finish, Sadie. I was wrong. Your mother helped me to see that. You'll have a family and kids one day, and we won't be involved if I keep up with my coldness."

My throat tightened.

"I ignored you for selfish reasons. My mind was always on winning because I didn't realize my full potential when I was Destin's age," Dad confessed.

I gaped at him in shock. "That's the reason?" I knew he had played briefly, but when he got injured and Mom fell pregnant, I thought he was okay with going into coaching.

He nodded, reaching for my hand. "I love you, Sadie. I was a fool, but I will never stop keeping the Panther's players away from you. They're all dogs, baby girl."

Dad laughed, and we all joined in, relaxing and enjoying each other's company.

* * *

The dinner with my family brought everything full circle, and I was happy to leave for a little getaway with my favorite person. Taking a private jet was even better. The lifestyle of a famous athlete's girlfriend wasn't so bad.

The cabin was two stories with a jacuzzi in the back I planned on relaxing in later. Elise couldn't drink, but I made up for the both of us and was already on my second one of the afternoon.

Elise side-eyed me. "Why are you so happy?"

"Because I am." I saw Destin and Sean laughing as they brought in the grocery bags.

Elise kicked off her heels, tucking underneath her legs. "Tell me the truth. Do you really like Destin?"

I laced my fingers around my glass. "I do."

"Well, happiness looks great on you both." Elise patted my arm.

"Yes, and my parents love him."

"All parents love Destin."

"He's not what I thought initially. He's different with me."

Elise leaned over to grab the snack tray. "You're shocked."

"Honestly, yes, because what he shows the world is a jerk who only cares about himself."

"Until he got with you." Elise held the tray out to me, and I took a sandwich.

"We're happy."

"I'm glad for you."

"Do you think doing all this for a job and money is stupid?"

Elise gulped her water. "Hell, no. Get what you can from this and double it into a bigger bag."

Destin, Sean, and I went on a small hike for the rest of the afternoon, leaving Elise to rest in bed. Later that evening, Elise and I cooked crusted calamari, salad, baked cod, and pasta.

"What are you planning to do tomorrow?" Destin asked as he pulled up a chair beside me at the table.

"Maybe we can go into town shopping?"

"I was thinking we could stay in tomorrow."

"What would your plan be?" I cooed, feeding him some of my baked cod.

"Please save that for the bedroom. Trying to eat here," Elise said, scrunching up her face.

"Yo! Get your wife, bro." Destin motioned at Sean to get Elise away from him.

Sean grinned. "She's fine."

"See? My man knows what's up," Elise taunted, kissing Sean.

"I'm going to be sick now," Destin jested.

He and Elise went back and forth until dinner was over. Afterward, we watched a movie until Elise wanted to go to bed, and then Destin and I went out to the jacuzzi.

Wearing my new two-piece bathing suit, I sank into the steaming water and curled up next to him. "Feels good here."

"Come sit on my lap."

"Sitting on your lap will lead to other things."

"I hope so." Destin extended his hand to help me to straddle his lap.

"Sadie?"

"Yes?"

"You're sexy as fuck."

I looked into his eyes as I wrapped my arms around his neck. "Thank you."

"All this for me." Destin rubbed my ass, making me moan.

"All of me."

He slipped a finger between my thong and rubbed my clit. "Damn, I am a lucky man."

I arched my back as he pushed his fingers in and out of my slick entrance. "Yes. Yes, you are."

Chapter 10

Destin

Fifth Month

My ability to think straight went out the window when Sadie stepped into her bedroom wearing only a trench coat. She'd called me over for dinner and a movie to celebrate me being back on the field and her getting the props in the media for being named the top physical therapist in Tennessee. For once, it was nice to see my name linked to positive news and hearing how proud my parents were now that the team was preparing for the World Cup in Mexico.

Soft music played in the background, and I took in her bedroom with plush pillows on the large queen size bed. Lit candles made the room smell like sandalwood.

Sadie took me by the hand, swishing her hips in a sexy little dance. She moved close, gripping my chin and kissing me deeply, swirling her tongue with mine.

I palmed her ass and then smacked it. "Fucking sexy, baby."

"Sexy and willing. Come here and let me feed you."

"Is this all mine?" I motioned to her naked body.

Sadie tugged off my shirt and reached down to unbuckle my pants. "It belongs to you, Destin."

I pushed the trench coat off her shoulders and peppered kisses down her jaw and neck. Caressing her soft skin, I walked her to the bed and pushed her down. "So fucking sexy."

Dropping my boxers, I leaned over and ran my fingers across her pussy and between her slit. She spread her legs wider, locking her hands around my neck as I dipped two fingers inside.

"Feed me, baby."

"Yes," she cooed as I lowered my face to smell her sweet essence.

Circling my tongue, I placed her legs over my shoulders. "I love your taste, Sadie."

Sadie arched her back off the bed, trying to control my movements with her hands on my head.

Teasing her clit, I pulled back with a gleam in my eyes. "So hot and ready, baby."

"Let me up, Destin."

I growled. "So this your show, Sadie?"

She grinned. "You can't have all the fun."

"Do your thing, baby," I said, stretching out on the bed with my hands behind my head.

Sadie glided her hand over my chest, rolling her thumb over my nipple as she took the tip of my cock into her mouth.

I sucked in a breath at the sensation of her warm, wet mouth on the sensitive head. "Baby, you're fucking my head up."

Smirking at my statement, innocent Sadie left the

building, and Sadie the vixen entered the bedroom. She swirled and teased me with her tongue, driving me insane as I pumped in and out of her mouth.

"That's enough, baby," I grunted, knowing I was on the edge.

I took her nipple in my mouth, sucking hard as I lined myself up with her opening.

"Mmm...Ow." She tensed at my intrusion as I bottomed out inside her.

"You're a big girl. You can handle me, baby."

Sadie rocked her hips back and forth. "Yes! Fuck, Destin."

"Keep your eyes open."

Digging her nails into my shoulders, Sadie bounced in my lap. I gripped her hips as I pumped in and out, the wet sounds of her pussy driving me crazy. I'd give her anything she wanted, and she didn't even know it.

Flipping us over, I pushed deeper, swallowing her moan of pleasure as we kissed.

"Oh, Jesus, Destin. I'm about to come!"

"Keep your eyes on me."

Thrusting harder, I licked between her breasts and bit down gently on her nipple. I hooked my hand beneath her knee and hooked her leg over my hip to allow me to go even deeper. The headboard hit the wall as I pounded into her, sweat pouring down my chest.

I smacked her breast, twisting her nipple, and Sadie exploded, squirting all over my stomach.

"Oh shit!"

My hips jerk. "Fuck, I'm about to blow."

Crashing our lips together, I let go, roaring my pleasure as I released.

* * *

I invited Sadie to my place for the weekend. Sadie was in her element, wearing one of my white long-sleeved shirts while she carried out calls with potential clients.

After finishing my workout for the day, I was going out for drinks with the boys so she could catch up on the work she'd missed while wrapped up in my media circus of a career.

Sadie closed the laptop and stretched her arms.

I came up behind her and kissed the back of her head. "How did it go?"

"Good. I'm looking at a potential space to open a practice."

"Nice. I like a boss that takes charge." I lifted her hand to my lips. "I'll be back."

"Where are you going?"

"To the club."

"Without me?"

"You were working. I didn't want to disturb you."

"Give me a minute. I can change."

I side-eyed her. "Sure you can hang?"

"Boy, I can probably out-drink you." She jumped up from the couch, strolling to my bedroom to change clothes.

I liked that Sadie wasn't stuck up, and she clearly wasn't after my money. I could joke and be myself around her. Sadie was also cool when women threw themselves at me, often laughing it off. That told me Sadie was a woman who had confidence in herself.

"Ready to go." Sadie emerged from the bedroom wearing high-waisted pants, a leather jacket over a halter top, and heels.

I yanked her to me. "Maybe we should stay. That ass is calling my name."

"You can take them off me when we get back. Come on." Twisting from my arms, she picked up her purse, leaving me to gaze at her rounded ass in awe.

"Gonna bite that ass later," I promised.

"What did you say?" Sadie quirked an eyebrow from the door.

"Nothing, baby."

"Yeah, right." Sadie giggled.

I locked up behind us, and we climbed into the waiting car. Since we were drinking, I didn't want to drive and have another police incident.

"Thanks, Tyler." I thanked the driver.

"No problem, sir." Tyler closed the door behind us and climbed behind the wheel.

Sadie reached for my hand, linking our fingers, smiling at me.

We arrived at the club ten minutes later, and I told Tyler not to worry about getting out. "We'll call you when we're ready."

"I'll be here, Mr. Gray."

"Thanks, T."

"It looks crowded," Sadie observed.

"You scared to hang with me, baby?"

"Please!" she snorted. "You better hope you can keep up with me."

She stepped out of the car, clasping my arm as we headed for the club.

"Sadie, can we have your autograph?"

Sadie looked shocked. "Um, *my* autograph? Don't you mean Destin's autograph?"

"No. You're one of our girl crushes. Independent

woman. Sexy. And your own boss." The girls high-fived each other.

"I'm just like you, ladies. A down-to-earth working woman."

"Baby, you're too modest. I can take the picture for you," I offered, taking the camera from them.

"Thanks!" both girls answered, standing on either side of Sadie. I took two pictures and a live video, then waited for Sadie to finish autographing their hands.

When we finally made it inside, the DJ announced my entrance over the speaker. "We got the big homie in the house! Destin Gray!"

The club-goers raised their hands and screamed.

Nudging through a few women trying to grab me, I pulled Sadie in front of me up to the VIP section where the others were waiting.

"We hanging with pregnant women now!" I joked, seeing Elise sitting in Sean's lap.

"Hush, Destin. I needed to make sure you play nice tonight," Elise teased, sticking her tongue out at me.

I turned to Sadie. "Baby, you want a drink?"

"Whatever you're having."

"Gotcha, sweet cheeks."

"I guess that contract did work in your favor," Sadie said with a smirk.

"Worry about that baby not coming out with your big head," I taunted.

Elise laughed and punched me in the arm as Sadie sat next to me on the couch.

"To us." We clinked glasses.

I glanced around, noticing how some women tried to impress me by bending over close to our section, but no one turned me on like Sadie with her thick, sexy ass twerking on my lap.

I clasped a hand around her waist and whispered, "Keep making moves like that, and I'll be bending your ass over."

"I'm letting my hair down tonight."

"Don't show out."

"Or what?"

I winked. "Try it and see."

I watched her get up and gulp the rest of the drink. She turned to Bobby's girlfriend, Racquel, and the two women started dancing, giving us a show. Sadie removed her jacket, and her tits were perky beneath her shirt, her nipples hard and ready for me to suck. I adjusted myself, my dick ready to burst out of my pants. The music changed to Thique by Beyonce, and all the women, including Sadie and Racquel, flooded the dance floor.

"Judging by the smile on your face, that woman is keeping you happy," Bobby said, refilling his glass. "She's got you wrapped around her finger."

"Fuck you."

"I get it, bro. Women like that are a dime a dozen."

"Too soon to love her, you think?"

I shook my head. "I can't answer that."

"Racquel stole my money last night after I went to sleep."

"Why the fuck did you bring her with you tonight?"

"Her pussy's good."

"Man, you're ignorant."

"Are you ready for the World Cup?"

"Yeah. I want people to know I can pull this off again and not by luck."

"Leave the doubters where they are. We know you have the skills." Bobby stuck his fist out for a bump.

"Appreciate you, bro."

"Brothers for life."

The rest of the evening, we laughed, danced, and enjoyed our friends for the last time before we flew to Mexico for the World Cup.

Chapter 11

Sadie

World Cup weeks afterward

Bright sun beamed down on the field. I listened to the announcer tell everyone that one of the players on the Brazil team was okay after injuring his leg in a collision with another player. As the captain,

I'd trained for this moment for four years, noting the best players on each team and their weaknesses. Today, we were up two to one, but we already had a few players being treated by Sadie for minor injuries. Coach was on the sideline, barking orders as usual. I wiped the sweat from my brow and took slow breaths.

"Come on, bro. You ready to repeat?" Bobby called, jogging over.

I cracked my knuckles. "World Champions all day long."

I caught the eye of the Brazilian goalie, who smirked at me. I couldn't wait to turn that smile upside down.

"Destin, you ready?" Adam yelled from across the field.

I got into position, ready to end all the naysayers and take the trophy. The ball came to me, and I beat a Brazilian defender, keeping control of the ball. I felt like I was floating on air. Another player tried to steal, but I passed the ball to Adam, who dribbled it toward the Brazilian goal before passing it back to me. I whipped around another defender, glancing up to sight the goal and the position of the goalie. Sending up a prayer, I whipped the ball in, sending it over the goalie's head and into the corner of the net.

The entire stadium erupted in excitement as the US won the World Cup. Bobby and Adam raced over, picking me up. I threw my hands in the air as Coach, and the rest of the team ran onto the field to celebrate. The announcer gave a play-by-play of the winning goal, and I looked out at the crowd, wishing Sadie wasn't stuck in the back. Finally, the trophy was in my hands, and I raised it in the air triumphantly before passing it off to my teammates.

"A World Cup Champion once again, Destin! How do you feel?" a reporter inquired.

"Feels like I won the lotto," I joked.

He laughed. "Anything you want to say to the fans back home?"

"Thank you to our fans, the Panthers organization, and my lucky charm, Sadie Myers."

"Once again, our Champions, led by the Captain of the Tennessee Panthers, Destin Gray." The reporter looked into the camera, and the entire team held up their index fingers in a number one.

Simon let the champagne cork rip as we walked into the locker rooms, and we all jumped up and down in excitement. I scanned the document Simon passed me detailing the extension of my contract for another five years.

"What do you say we try for another win in four years?" Simon asked.

"Long as Sadie's here, we have a deal."

"It was her idea."

Sadie ran into my arms and planted a kiss on my mouth. "Congrats, captain."

Squeezing her tight, I chuckled as I swung her around. I placed her back on her feet and tugged her into the closet next to the locker room for privacy.

Pressing my body against her, I kissed her deeply, moaning into her mouth. "Kissing you is my favorite thing to do."

"Proud of you."

"I'm ready to be alone with you."

"A few more pictures and interviews, and then we can go back to the hotel." Sadie waggled her eyebrows and gave me a saucy grin. "Oh, and Simon deposited the money in my account."

"Good. Now, let's have our own private celebration."

"Not in here," Sadie giggled, trying to keep her clothes from coming off.

"Baby, you can't leave me hanging like this."

Glancing down at my hard dick, Sadie grinned, pecked me on the lips, and turned to leave the closet.

"Always making me work hard," I groaned.

Sadie stuck her head back in the room. "It's always worth it, though."

* * *

Sadie adjusted my tie and leaned forward, kissing me on the cheek as we arrived at the sports award show. Sadie wore a light blue, low-cut V-neck gown that tied in the back, showing off her curves. At first, I protested her wearing it because I wanted to take it off and forget about the damn award show.

Opening my car door, I stepped out first, waving and smiling to the crowd. I extended my palm toward Sadie to help her out of the car, and she winked at me as I pulled her close.

"You two look beautiful," Morian, my new publicist, motioned us toward the red carpet.

"This is huge. I've never gone to a sports award show." Sadie took in the fans and photographers calling my name.

"Get used to it." I squeezed her tight.

"Destin! Over here!" A photographer called my name.

Morian stepped forward to direct the chaos as more athletes showed up. A few of my teammates approached, and we shook up and posed with our girlfriends.

"Destin and Sadie! Right here!" a photographer I'd given an interview to last year called.

"No questions tonight, please," Morian requested politely.

As usual, the host was a retired athlete, and Sadie was excited to see her favorite sports personalities. Grasping her hand, I escorted her inside, and Morian led us to the table near the stage. I was nominated for two awards: Favorite Athlete and Goal of the Year. The event had performances and food for us to enjoy since it lasted for two hours.

"Are you excited?" Sadie rubbed her hand across my thigh.

I draped my arm over the back of her chair and leaned in to kiss her on the cheek. "Yeah. But no matter if I win or lose, I get to take you home."

"We have the number one star in the building tonight," the announcer said.

The spotlight landed on me, and I raised my hand in acknowledgment.

"First award for MVP of The Year goes to Destin Gray!"

I was shocked. Sadie grasped my chin and pulled me in for a quick kiss. I stood and jogged up the stairs to accept my award.

"Wow, are you sure this is for me?" I joked.

The crowd laughed and clapped, and I saw some teammates up out of their chairs.

"All I can say is I'm grateful for the support and for the best thing to come into my life. Sadie, you're the only one for me." I stared down at her, ready to put a baby inside her. "Thank you to the voters and my family and team for their support," I finished, walking back down the stairs to join Sadie at my table.

The after-party was non-stop. Sadie cut loose, dancing in front of me and shaking her ass while I held both awards up with a cigar in my mouth.

"Fuck it up, baby."

Sadie smirked and circled her hips seductively, which made my dick hard.

I leaned forward, nuzzling my nose into her neck. "Keep moving like that, and I'm going to fuck you right here."

"I wouldn't object." Sadie turned to face me, wrapping her arms around my waist.

I bent to kiss her. "Ready to go?"

"Yes, more than ready."

"Shit, you're sexy as fuck."

"I hope you feel that way in nine months," Sadie said.

The music was so loud that I thought I'd misheard her. I moved my hand over her stomach. "You're pregnant?"

She nodded. "A few weeks."

"Seriously?"

"Yes. How do you feel about that?"

"Damn, I'm going to be a daddy."

"Destin, are you sure about doing this with me? Because I can handle it on my own," Sadie challenged.

"Fucking right, I'm sure. You are the most important thing to me, Sadie. I love you."

"I love you, too." Sadie leaned against my chest.

I was ready to take her home and enjoy her fully away from prying eyes. I took Sadie's hand and left the VIP section, notifying our security that we were ready to go.

"Why are you leaving so fast, Destin? The party's just getting started," Sadie giggled.

I paused long enough to throw her over my shoulder, and she squealed as I smacked her ass. I carried her outside, lowering her back to her feet as we reached the limo.

"From bad boy to daddy in one year." Sadie grinned up at me.

Lifting her hand, I kissed her palm and opened the door for her to climb in just as the paparazzi started to swarm around. My new life included a child and, hopefully, a wife. A woman I loved more than anything.

"Mr. Combs, are you excited about the new season?" a reporter asked as I slid in beside Sadie.

"I'm excited about a lot of things, but soccer is second on the list right now."

He pushed the microphone closer to my face. "Are you hinting that wedding plans are in your future?"

I ignored his question and shut the door behind me, chuckling at him trying to get a scoop.

Sadie glanced over her shoulder. "What was that about?"

"Just me taking the high road."

"I like this new Destin."

"I feel like I have the biggest prize of all."

Sadie pressed her lips to mine. "We both came out on top this time."

Taking Sadie on as my physical therapist was the best decision I'd ever made. "Scoring with Sadie," I mumbled into the kiss, rubbing her stomach.

Epilogue: Sadie

Five years later

"DJ, don't get dirty, baby," I walked onto the field, shaking my head at how DJ wanted to be like his dad at all times.

"Mommy, I want to get dirty." DJ laughed as his father kicked the ball toward him.

I rubbed my stomach as our daughter kicked me. She was due in four months. "Destin, you promised not to get him tired and dirty."

Destin ran around with DJ. "Baby, relax. We're good."

Lifting my wrist, I checked the time on my watch. "We have twenty minutes to get to the event."

Destin walked over to me, smoothing a hand over my belly. He wrapped his arm around my waist, drawing me to his chest. "Are you excited?"

"Yes, but I would be more excited if our child didn't show up dirty and sweaty."

He chuckled, clasping my hand. "Come on, DJ. We have to go."

After his retirement, Destin started an organization to bring soccer to his local community and create scholarships for boys and girls to get a start in school. Bringing in support from his teammates and the Panthers, he opened locations in Los Angeles, Atlanta, and Detroit.

DJ ran over with the ball. "But, Dad."

Destin rubbed his head. "We can finish after the event, buddy."

I loved the relationship Destin had with our son. No more the bad boy, out partying and getting into trouble every other day. He was now a husband and father, ensuring carpool was scheduled months in advance.

"No buts. Your mommy is about to celebrate a big accomplishment."

I smiled at our son. "Because of you, I decided to open my practice, DJ."

"Really?" DJ stood between us, taking my hand.

I nodded. "Really."

Destin took the ball and held his other hand. Walking to our waiting limo, Destin helped DJ into his car seat.

"Mommy's opening a new business." Destin handed the ball back and helped me next. "Congrats, Mommy."

"Thank you, baby."

* * *

"Ladies and gentlemen, we are here to celebrate the opening of Gray Myers Physical Therapy Center," the director of the center, Carl Sinclair, announced before passing the microphone to me.

I stood next to him, Destin, my parents, Kelly, and some of the players from the organization. "Thank you, Carl. It's been a long time coming, but I can't thank my parents and the Panthers enough for supporting me."

"You go, girl!" Kelly yelled into the microphone, making everyone laugh.

"To the most amazing husband who stayed up late with our son while I worked on my vision. Destin, I love you from the bottom of my heart."

"You made it easy, baby," Destin whispered in my ear.

"On the count of three, we will cut the ribbon," Carl said.

I nodded, passing the microphone to Destin to hold. I stood in front of the two-level building I'd built from the ground up with the money from the contract with Destin. He'd also invested in the building and got me most of my client referrals.

"One, two, three!" Everybody yelled as the ribbon was cut.

* * *

I hope you enjoyed Destin and Sadie's story.

Check the sneak peek of **"Something Borrowed"** on the next page.

Follow my standalone, opposites attract, age gap, military romance **"Exposed"** https://books2read.com/u/bQyYZe.

Are you a fan of sports romance? Then download one-night stand, billionaire romance **"Refuel"** https://books2read.com/u/boDyDA.

Follow it up with workplace, sports romance **"Pressure"** https://books2read.com/u/3Ly1r7.

If you love romantic comedy, fake relationships, enemies to lovers, find it here, **"Something Gained."** Click the link here https://books2read.com/u/baGLYy.

My stories of friends finding love started with the Heart of Stone series, which includes a host of characters and family. **"Broken, Book 1 Emery and Jackson,"** a sports, one-night stand, workplace romance, is here: https://books2read.com/u/3LoelX

Then you can continue with a fun side story of Emery and Jackson with a Valentine's Day short here: https://books2read.com/u/4jAypY

Jordan, her best friend's story, continues here in **"Rebirth, Book 2,"** a single dad, widow billionaire romance here: https://books2read.com/u/ba2OMx

* * *

Please also check out a second-chance workplace romance here, **"Renew, Book 4"** https://books2read.com/u/4NXyPG, with a host of characters intertwined.

Follow Desiree and Gabriel in **"Temptation,"** a standalone contemporary, sports, curvy girl romance. Check it out here https://books2read.com/u/mle1Vv

Check out dark mafia romance here that started my journey with Antonio and Sabrina in **"Ruthless, Book 1"** https://books2read.com/u/4AxKLo

The relationship continues in **"Savage, Book 2"** as they get to know each other and their families: https://books2read.com/u/bpED6g

Antonio and Sabrina have more work to do in **"Beast, Book 3"** right here: https://books2read.com/links/ubl/4AxKOd

* * *

Did you know Janice and Carlo have a book? Grab this dark mafia romance with emotional scars and betrayal right here: https://books2read.com/u/b6je6M

Any fans of forbidden romance in politics? Check out **"Mutual Agreement"** https://books2read.com/u/mgzzWX a steamy romance.

Have you checked out **"She's All I Need?"** Click here https://books2read.com/u/49lkeW a sports, opposites attract romance.

What about dark romance with everything from steamy romance, opposites attract, suspense, thriller, celebrity, and more? **"Stolen, Book 1"** https://books2read.com/u/mvZlgV

Don't miss the follow-up Joaquin and Sofia's story in **"Saved, Book 2"** https://books2read.com/u/4DWwLd

The conclusion for Joaquin and Sofia comes full circle in **"Betrayed"** here: https://books2read.com/u/4A5LGp

* * *

Catch up with your favorite characters in this holiday short romance, including spoilers. **"Holiday collection"** here https://books2read.com/u/bzd59G

For small-town, single mom stories, check out **"Until Serena"** https://books2read.com/u/mej8vr.

Always fun when you love billionaire romances, so check in with **"Cocky Catcher,"** a sports romance, enemies to lovers here: https://books2read.com/u/bOxNgJ.

Some familiar characters show up in **"Bossy**

Billionaire," a workplace, enemies-to-lovers romance here: https://books2read.com/u/mvZoDq

All curvy girl, plus size romance lovers get into **"I Deserve His Love,"** a standalone, second chance romance here: https://books2read.com/u/mVrGwP

The fantasy romance readers look no further than a **"Red Light District,"** a curvy girl, fling romance here: https://books2read.com/u/m2RQ6G

Something Earned: Romantic Comedy Book 2

A workplace, friends to lovers, romantic comedy.

Kianna has worked hard and knows she deserves a promotion at the music label, despite what all the naysayers in her life say.

Caleb has gone above and beyond to prove he can handle more work responsibilities. What he's not sure he's ready to handle is competing with Kianna for a job.

A promotion is up for grabs, but only one can have it. With ex-lovers, a relationship blurring the lines between coworkers, good friends, and lovers, Kianna and Caleb have a lot on their minds.

Can they ignore the outside distractions and focus on what matters, or will they jeopardize what could be the best thing to ever happen to them?

Nicco TN Seal Security Book 3

Charlie, a well-respected researcher, knows everyone has secrets, but it changes everything when she uncovers secrets at work.

Soon, she finds herself in a terrible predicament of her own making and needs to enlist the help of a handsome former Navy Seal and his security team. But going toe-to-toe with the Mob proves much more dangerous than anyone expected.

Can Nicco and his team keep her out of harm's way, or are the Mob's tentacles too long and well-connected?

Reading Order of Heart of Stone Series

Heart of Stone Book 1 Emery and Jackson
https://books2read.com/u/boWPAV
Heart of Stone Book 1.5
https://payhip.com/b/kWg7
Heart of Stone Book 2 Jordan and Damon
https://books2read.com/u/ba2OMx
Heart of Stone Book 3.5 Bottoms Up
https://payhip.com/b/HGP1
Heart of Stone Book 3 Angela and Brent
https://books2read.com/u/31rx9l
Heart of Stone Book 4 Jessica and Joseph
https://books2read.com/u/4NXyPG

Reading Order of Antonio and Sabrina Universe

The Early Years-A Prequel
https://books2read.com/u/49Zjnw
Ruthless Struck In Love Book 1
https://books2read.com/u/4AxKLo
Savage Struck In Love Book 2
https://books2read.com/u/bpED6g
Beast Struck In Love Book 3
https://books2read.com/u/3LpgdJ
Janice and Carlo Captivated By His Love
https://books2read.com/u/b6je6M
Brutal Struck In Love Book 4
https://books2read.com/u/4NQyE9
Stolen-Fuertes Mafia Cartel Book 1
https://books2read.com/u/mvZlgV
Saved-Fuertes Mafia Cartel Book 2
https://books2read.com/u/4DWwLd
Redemption Struck In Love Book 5
https://books2read.com/u/b5kZ8O
Betrayal- Fuertes Mafia Cartel Book 3
https://books2read.com/u/4A5LGp

What's Next?

Want to know what happens next?

Follow me on my website to catch the next release.

Reviews are the lifeblood of the publishing world. They're read, appreciated, and needed.

Please consider taking the time to leave a few words on your review platform of choice.

Sign up for updates and sneak peaks at the site below. www.chiquitadennie.com

Catalog Releases

Catalog Releases

By Chiquita Dennie:

The Early Years—A Prequel Short Story

Ruthless: Struck in Love 1

Savage: Struck in Love 2

Beast: Struck in Love 3

Brutal: Struck in Love 4

Redemption: Struck in Love 5

Broken Book 1 (Emery & Jackson)

Heart Of Stone Book 1.5 Emery & Jackson A Valentine's Day Short

Janice and Carlo: Captivated by His Love

Rebirth Book 2 (Jordan and Damon)

Temptation

Reveal Book 3 (Angela and Brent)

Cocky Catcher

Bossy Billionaire

Bottoms Up Heart of Stone, Book 3.5 (Jessica and Joseph Short)

Love Shorts: A Collection of Short Stories
Stolen: Fuertes Mafia Cartel Book 1
Exposed (Salvation Society Novel)
Saved: Fuertes Mafia Cartel Book 2
Refuel (A Driven World Novel)
Pressure (A Driven World Novel)
Until Serena (HEA World Novel)
Renew Book 4 (Jessica and Joseph)
She's All I Need
Red Light District (A Fantasy Romance Short)
Aydin: TN Seal Security Book 1
Nasir: TN Seal Security Book 2
Betrayed: Fuertes Mafia Cartel Book 3
Something Gained (A Romantic Comedy Book 1)
Torn: The Carrington Cartel Book 1
Claim: The Carrington Cartel Book 2

Thank you so much for reading, and if you enjoyed the crazy ride and decide to leave a review, we'd truly appreciate the support.

About the Author

Chiquita Dennie is an author of Contemporary, Romantic Suspense, Erotic, and Women's Fiction.

Chiquita lives in Los Angeles, CA. Before writing contemporary romance, she worked in the entertainment industry on notable TV shows such as the Dr. Phil Show, Tyra Banks Show, American Idol, and Deal or No Deal. But her favorite job is the one she's now doing, full-time writing romance.

A Best-Selling Author and Award-winning Film-maker, her first short film, "Invisible," was released in the summer of 2017, screened in multiple festivals, and won Best Short Film. She also hosts a podcast that showcases the latest in the beauty, business, and community called "Moscato and Tea." Her debut release, "Struck in Love," with Antonio and Sabrina, has opened a new avenue of writing she loves.

If you want to know when the next book will be released, please visit my website at http://www.chiquitadennie.com, where you can sign up to receive an email for my next release.

Acknowledgments

I want to dedicate this to my team that helps me behind the scenes, from my editors, test readers, graphic designers, and so on. I truly appreciate each of you for keeping me on my toes.

304 Publishing Company

We showcase authors writing African American, Interracial, Women's Fiction, Urban Romance, Erotic, and Contemporary Romance novels. Along with Thriller, Suspense, Poetry, Beauty, and Style Books. Thank you for taking the time to visit. Join our mailing list to stay updated with new releases and blog posts.